To "Enjoy"

Demon's Kiss

By

Laura Hawks

Trip -
Pleasure meeting
you at RomCon 2016
Laura Hawks

Copyright © 2012 Laura Hawks

All rights reserved

No part of this book may be reproduced in any form or by any electronic or mechanical means, including information storage and retrieval systems, without permission in writing from the publisher, except by a reviewer who may quote brief passages in a review.

The characters and events portrayed in this book are fictitious. Any similarity to real persons, living or dead is coincidental and not intended by the author.

Cover Art by Kristy Charbonneau

Edited by Jacquelynn Gagne

Acknowledgements

I would like to take a moment to thank a couple of people for helping me get this book to all of you. Liam... I could not have written this or had the courage to submit this if not for you and the faith you have in me. You are a great friend and I love you, no matter where in the world you are.

I would also like to thank Anthony for being there for me and listening to me complain about anything and everything as well as for supporting me and unknowingly, letting me try some phrases that I was not entirely sure would work. Ant...you are a great accomplice, a dear friend and a wonderful partner in crime. Love you lots.

Dennis, thanks for helping and encouraging me in every way. I love all you do to help support my dream.

Last but by no means least, I would like to thank all my friends and family who said I could do this and it was worth the effort and who told me they were proud of me regardless of whether or not I succeeded. The encouragement you have shown has been the backbone to keep me going. I love you all.

Thank you for your patronage!
After you have enjoyed reading this novel, I would greatly appreciate it if you would leave a review at Amazon and/or Goodreads.

Prologue

Cloudy mists swirled around her as ethereal fingers caressed an adumbration she couldn't yet comprehend. The opaque fog rolled along the ground. Its gossamer threads spinning and cresting as if a wave on an ocean. Nothing was tangible. It was hidden by the diaphanous strands that shimmered about her. Then the mists cleared. An image of the Gem of Power Dagger formed in her dream and her eyes snapped open. "Oh Gods, no!"

Clarissa ran to the dagger, unthinkingly grabbing it. Her powers of premonition kicked in immediately. She began to convulse and dropped to the floor. Her eyes were shaded white. She saw a large creature. He was nearing the cave where she had buried the other piece of the gem. He was going to find it and have access to the power the stone carried with it. Did he realize it was not whole? Did he realize the power could not fully be obtained unless it was? Did he know she as guardian, had the other piece?

Her vision flashed to the future. It showed a battle with a strikingly handsome man who stood by her side fighting the demon. They were together. She awoke, free from the perceptions the dagger showed her and gasped. She had a journey ahead of her. She had to get the piece of gem she had buried before he ever got near it.

*****

The judge and executioner of rebel demons stared into the fire. He sipped his meal and reflected over the events of the day. He enjoyed the moment of peace, no matter how short lived it ended up being. As he lifted the goblet to his lips, a strong current ripped through his body. It was so intense the goblet dropped, spilling the liquid contents everywhere. He gripped the arms of his chair, managing to calm his mind enough to concentrate on the disruption in the cosmos.

"The Gem of Power!"

He sprang from his seat and began to frantically pace the hall.

"Why now, after all this time?"

He stopped pacing. As he cocked his head, he concentrated on the gem. He was still in awe that it might have resurfaced after so long. The perceptions were hazy but he saw a beautiful blonde woman as she hiked through mountains. He recognized them to be in South America. He realized she was a wolf shifter. As scenes paraded through his head, he instantly knew where to go find the woman. She seemed to be the key.

Chapter One

Clarissa heaved her backpack onto her shoulders after she teleported to the base of the Pakaraima Mountains of Guyana. There were located southwest in the South American country which shared its borders with Brazil and Venezuela. Due to the denseness of the forests, she had to hike the rest of the way to the tallest peak of the range, Mount Roraima. If not she risked teleporting into a tree or boulder. Slinging the backpack over her shoulder, Clarissa hoped she was not too late to prevent the demon from obtaining the portion of gem hidden there.

She moved through the trees and brush, wiping a sweaty hand across her brow. She took a sip of water from her supplies. She continued the trek, only stopping to test the air.

An unfamiliar scent wafted across the breeze to her. The smell indicated the creature was still a couple of miles up ahead. It was undeniably demon. Her eyes narrowed and her stomach dropped.

Clarissa shifted quickly to wolf form in order to move through the brush faster. She stopped only a short distance from him before shifting back to human. The guardian called forth her sword and had it at the ready. She was unsure what good it would do considering the amount of power that surrounded this creature. Stepping out of the brush into the clearing she saw him, sitting, waiting. Instantly, Clarissa realized this was the man from her visions. This was the one who stood by her side to fight the demon intent on taking the stone.

Gods, the man before her was gorgeous. He had dark hair and haunting pale blue eyes. An aquiline nose set in the middle of a face with a strong, slightly whiskered jaw. His shoulders were wide. Even though he had on a crisp, white button down shirt, one could tell he was ripped underneath from the pull of material across his chest. The sleeves were rolled up and she was surprised that the shirt didn't tear at the seams as tight as it was on him. He reeked of ancient wisdom and knowledge. Although he didn't look any more than thirty five, she could sense he was infinitely older.

*****

Azamel was so sure the gem had been lost over the centuries. Now it resurfaced its quintessence strong. He traced the woman's presence to Guyana, South America and teleported to a spot slightly ahead of her. He made sure he had a clear view of her progress up the steep peak. He sat down on a fallen down tree stump and waited. The executioner smiled mysteriously as she walked closer. Azamel could sense the wolf's discomfort, nervousness and suspicion. He knew she was the one he sought but decided not to play his hand just yet. Waiting for her to make the first move, Mel continued to watch her.

She moved with a beautiful grace. Her long, curly blond locks framed a small heart-shaped face. Almost almond shaped orbs with long lashes framed emerald eyes. She had an inner beauty that radiated through her very being. She was younger than he anticipated but then were-wolves had a tendency to always look more youthful then they were. Knowing that, she was probably closer to thirty.

Clarissa was not one for delicacy so blatantly asked him, "What do you want?"

Azamel noticed the dipping sun as he waved a hand and a campfire appeared in front of him. The flames licked at the wood, giving the surrounding area a pleasant feel. "You can put that away wolf. I am not here to hurt you. If I wanted to do that, you would have been dead before you even saw me. Now take a seat so we can talk." He eyed the sword. "Or do I need to take that from you?"

The guardian bit her lower lip as she tried to decide what to do. He was most likely right. Had he wanted her dead, she would be. His strength of power was that impressive. Although a bit skittish, she was very aware of what was at stake. Clarissa never asked for this destiny she was burdened with. She was basically untrained for it but she did what she thought was right. Could she trust him? She lowered the sword, keeping it in her hand. She approached the far side of the fire and sat Indian style on the ground. Pulling her backpack off, she laid the sword across her lap.

"So talk. I will listen."

He chuckled softly but decided to humor her for now. He would not play any games about what he wanted.

"I am intrigued little one. I know why I am here and I know why that demon Xon is here. What fascinates me is why you are so intent on finding the stone?" He peered at her face intently.

Her features darkened because he had knowledge of the gem. "And what do you know of the stone? You want it for yourself?"

"That is also something I can achieve without you, Clarissa." At her shocked look, he added, "Yes I know who you are. However, you don't know who I am. My name is Azamel but most call me Mel. I can be your best friend in this quest-" He gave her a charming smile before he let his eyes harden and flash red for an instant, "or your greatest enemy."

Clarissa narrowed her eyes. "If you know who I am then you also know why I am after it. Or is your ignorance actually honest? I may be young, Mel, but I am not a fool. I will defend the stone or die trying to keep it away from you and any other creature foolish enough to search for it. Ally or enemy, I leave the choice to you."

"Careful, love, you have no idea who you are dealing with. I am not here to threaten nor hurt you. I do, however know a lot more about demons than you do and I suggest we work together on this, since I would hate for you to lose that pretty little head.

My interest is not so much in the gem but in the demon seeking it. I will not allow him to have it."

"I am always careful, Mel. For when one lets their guard down, one can easily be killed. I may not know much but I do know this. Why should I trust you? You claim to want to help me, yet all you have proven is you are mysterious and knowledgeable about the stone. You appear to know about me and yet pretend you do not know what my role is."

"I never asked for your trust and you may be wise to not trust me. I don't need to explain myself or my reasons to you. The fact that you are still alive and not dead at my feet should give you some indication of my peaceful intent. Currently, we have a more pressing problem. The demon is much closer to that stone than you are."

She remained silent, mulling over his words. Not knowing what he was about and telling her not to trust him was disconcerting at best. However, his blatant honesty had to be good for something and she was always taught to keep friends close and enemies closer. Since she really wasn't sure what category he fell into, considering him an enemy was her best course.

"What I am up against with this demon?"

He smiled as he sensed some capitulation from her, a small victory at best but still a victory. "Xon is a minor demon, bottom of the barrel scum. He has very few powers and that makes him dangerous. The stone would give him abilities needed to free himself from his bondage. His cruel master makes Xipe Totec, the Aztec god of torture look like Cupid. A caged animal is more dangerous than a powerful one in the wild. Xon will kill, maim and slaughter anything or anyone in his path to get what he wants. He has no compassion as it was quelled eons ago. What he lacks in efficacy, he makes up for in brute strength."

Clarissa watched as he sat back in a relaxed pose, while she debated, worried whether she could trust him. Oh well, she traipsed through it this far, might as well go one step further.

"Are you his master or his keeper?"

"I am neither, I am his judge and if necessary, his executioner."

She frowned slightly. He certainly had the macho thing going for him and at least he was easy on the eyes, not all scaly and bubbly with puss. The wolf in her still didn't trust him though. Of course by his own admission, he was one not to be trusted. The one thing Clarissa knew for sure was her vision of them seemingly fighting side by side. But what would happen after that? The stone was powerful and called to many. Could he resist it or would she, in the end, have to fight him too?

"Fine, you can travel with me for now but know this, I will protect the stone from you and anyone else who tries to take the powers it offers. I will do so even if it means my eventual death."

He sat very still, listening to her fiery declaration, her determination to protect the Gem of Power. Memories of what he had read about the stone started to shift through his mind. The tales told of a guardian to the stone, one sworn to protect it and its powers at all costs. The responsibility had been given to one family and from that family, one member from each generation was chosen to be its keeper. They couldn't use the powers for themselves but they had to ensure it did not get lost or stolen. He wondered because, her stance and fiery determination permeated of a protector. Azamel would have to be very careful how he treaded. Closing his emotions off to her as she was more perceptive than he had originally supposed, he addressed her again, "I propose a truce." He held out his hand, palm up in a sign of trust. "We are both after a similar goal and a partnership would benefit us." Looking her straight in the eyes. "I promise not to hurt you. the demon however, is another matter."

Utilizing her wolf senses, she took a deep breath and inhaled his scent. Truth was there but with a hint of something else. Not an outright lie but not full disclosure. Clarissa glanced at his hand, listened to his offer before she looked him in the eye. "Truce then, until you prove untrustworthy. Then I will slit your throat."

The guardian smiled sweetly and placed her hand in his. As their skin touched, she paled, her eyes glazed over, convulsing slightly she gripped his hand tighter, refusing to release him. Her premonition ability activated, she could see the demon getting close to the stone. She knew instinctively that he was ahead of them and he was not alone. He had sensed Azamel. He could tell the executioner was nearby and that made Xon call in some favors. Xon sent other demons toward the couple, to slow them down. Just in case, he had added a few additional surprises along the way. She could see each distraction the demon set in place, even the ones that were almost upon them. Gasping, she pushed his hand away and rolled to a defensive stance, shaking slightly from the strong vision.

"Hope you know how to fight, Mel, because it looks like we have company coming. Thanks to your friend."

She had no sooner finished her sentence when the loud crunch of underbrush gave way to ten Wendigos. They were gaunt to the point of emaciation, their desiccated skin pulled tautly over their skeleton. With an ash gray complexion and their eyes pushed deep into their sockets, the Wendigo looked like it was recently disinterred from the grave. What lips it had were tattered and bloody. Unclean and suffering from suppurations of the flesh, the Wendigo gave off a strange odor of decay and decomposition, of death and corruption.

"Well there goes any appetite I might have had! Phew, these guys stink! You take the five over there, I will get the rest." She glanced his way. "If you can handle it that is."

Dropping her backpack, she grabbed her sword tighter and moved towards those closest to her.

He got up flashing a staff with nine inch blades at each end into his hand. Mel twirled it around, grinning evilly. "Five? Oh that will not do, love." He jumped up, somersaulted and landed between the attackers with a *'fuck with me and die'* look. "Now now boys, do I really have to kill you?" He waved one hand in front of his nose. "I am not looking forward to getting your rank remains all over my shirt." The executioner shrugged. "Ah well, I can always buy another shirt, I suppose." Azamel twirled the staff faster, up over his head. With a battle cry, he slammed it down and decapitated two of the demons in one blow. Foul smelling goo flew everywhere. He turned to her with a grin. "Do try to keep up, love." He dropped down as a demon swung at him and thrust the staff up into its throat. "Come at me when I turn? Die you rank bastard!" Mel laughed with glee as he attacked with a vengeance.

Clarissa watched his jumping somersault out of the corner of her eye, mildly impressed. As one Wendigo reached for her, she dropped, swung out her legs and took his limbs out from under him. She chopped his head off in one quick, clean motion. Cart-wheeling over the corpse, she stood and swirled, ducking once more to avoid the majority of slushy remains that splashed towards her. "Stop jabbering and boring them to death, just kill them with your weapon." Clarissa saw three come towards her from all different directions. She did a split kick to push two of them back, while she simultaneously swung forward, splitting the other's skull in two.

"Gods, he is right. You guys do reek! Have you never heard of soap and water?" She turned her attention to the two she had kicked. While doing a jumping twirl, she took both of their heads with one arcing stroke.

Mel laughed at her. "Now who is doing the monologue?" He spotted a demon coming at her rear and blasted him in the back of the head. It sent remains flying all over her. "Fucking cowards, coming at a woman's back." He slammed the tip of the staff into the ground. He then kicked a demon in the chest sending it flying into another behind it. Mel jumped up and pressed the staff into the demons chest. He thrust his arms back, pushing the other side of the staff into a demon behind him. He flashed the staff away and a sword appeared in its place. Laughing like a kid in a toy store, Mel sliced through the demons as if they were not moving. Guts and ooze flew everywhere.

"Keeping up, love?"

"Just fine. How are your creaking bones managing, old man?" The guardian kicked back, pushing one away as she took the head of another. She then spun around quickly and removed the head of the one she just kicked. Noticing one about to go for Mel, she flipped to him and pushed him out of the way. She stabbed the Wendigo in the chest and pulled the sword up to be free again. "Glad to see you're having fun but keep your mind in the game." Dashing off, she attacked another. Jumping up, she flipped over its body and took its head with her in the move.

Azamel glared at her as the last Wendigo dropped dead to the ground. "Come, we do not have much time." Flashing the sword away, he moved up the mountain, his demon senses wide open, reading the land. The path would be treacherous at best.

Clarissa grabbed her backpack and followed him frowning, she wondered. *'When did he become the leader of this expedition.'* She tried to match the landscape to the visions she had. "Hey Gramps, maybe I should lead since I actually saw the traps being laid. I'm sorry, are you too macho to follow a woman?"

He did not appreciate her tone but decided to let it slide as they had more pressing matters. Mel stopped and turned towards her with a smirk. "Well then, who am I to stop you?" He waved his hand in a sweeping motion. "After you, Milady."

Clarissa skirted past him, chin held high. The ancient power he emitted was sometimes overwhelming and it did not help he was sexy as hell. She would not let him know how he affected her. "Try and keep pace. I cannot be waiting for you all night, you know." Hoisting her backpack tighter around her, the wolf took off at a light jog. She only stopped occasionally to machete her way past some vines. They had traveled quite a distance when the sun started to rise. She halted suddenly looking around. She remembered the vision she had. "Pits in three hundred meters."

He scanned the area. "Tell me, Ms. Expert, how would you get past this little hurdle hmm?"

"Here I thought you were the all knowledgeable one." She looked forward again and pondered. "Ever watch Tarzan cartoons?" Clarissa used her guardian powers of conjuring. She flashed in a grappling hook with a long rope before she turned to him. "I suggest you move back a touch more. I would hate to hurt you." Moving up closer, she used her telekinesis to move the brush aside revealing the extremely large pit. Swinging the hook, Clarissa let the rope expand slowly as she spun it, eye-balling her target before she released the grapple. The hook grabbed onto the large limb, twirling around it. She pulled on rope with all her strength to make sure it was tight enough as she smirked at him. "Do try and keep up."

Hoisting herself, she swung over the hidden pit, landing safely on the other side before flinging the rope to him. Mel chuckled as he admired her skills and feisty demeanor. "Very impressive, love, but there is one thing you need to remember about us old people. We are lazy." He held both hands in front of him and moved them slightly up. As his hands raised, the ground started to tremble and the pit began to fill up from the bottom.

Her mouth dropped in surprise as she had sensed he was powerful but Damn! When the ground was level, he walked over the area with a smug expression as he whistled a cheery tune. When he passed her, the demon enforcer winked. He then disappeared through the underbrush.

Here she was being arrogant to someone who could wipe the floor with her in one hand, blow his nose with the other and think nothing of either. She swallowed. Oh well, she was not about to change. Clarissa had a duty to fulfill and her sarcasm and bitterness were all she had left in this world. Mel would just have to deal or strike her dead. Turning quickly, she flashed the grapple hook and rope away. *'If nothing else, I will let him fix the next trap first before I do anything.'*

Azamel focused intently on the surroundings, paid attention to each creak, rustle and scrape, while she followed behind, silent, keeping close and as alert he was. As he stepped over a fallen branch, a very faint click reached his ears. "Get down!"

Chapter Two

Mel grabbed her arm pulling her to the ground. At the same time he conjured a shield around them. A massive board had sprung from the earth. Hundreds of poisoned spikes repelled in all directions, hoping to find its target in soft flesh. He protected her with his body, tucked her head against his chest with one hand while the other kept the shield in place.

She could feel the power he generated, heard the spikes hit the invisible wall at a blinding speed, a fierce staccato against the force field. Her body pressed under him, his scent assailed her. She closed her eyes as she breathed his intoxicating aroma in deeply.

When at last the assault ended, Mel dropped the barrier and lifted his head. He looked her over to see if she was harmed, only to notice how soft her body had felt beneath his. He was surprised how delicious her fragrance was in his nostrils. His hands quickly roamed her body, checked her for wounds and his touch sent an unexpected heat through both of them. *'What the hell was wrong with this picture? This was neither the time nor the place and probably not the person he should be getting all hot and bothered over.'* He cleared his throat and moved to get up.

Clarissa rolled out from under him, quickly stood and surveyed the damage. "I did not see this one in my vision. Thank you," she grumbled softly. She shook slightly as she looked at him. "Are you hurt? I would just pat you down as well but would hate for you to think I was making a move on you or something that would make you want to kill me." Without waiting for an answer, she started to walk down the path, her focus on the landmarks. She needed to calm her nerves from being so close to his body and the effect he seemed to suddenly have on her, even momentarily.

Azamel frowned slightly as he watched her walk ahead. *'What the hell? She must have felt that, no way she didn't. The little wolf is not as immune to me as she pretends to be.'* What bothered him more, he was not unaffected by her either. He rubbed his hand over his face and took off after her. He kept silent as he thought about what just happened.

Clarissa stopped again as she turned towards him. She decided to give in a little. ultimately, he did just save her life. "I know of at least one more trap. I cannot guarantee that is all of them, because I did not see the last one. I would suggest we move a bit further before we rest a bit. There is a clearing up ahead. About a mile and it is by a lake, so fresh water."

"Lead the way then." He materialized a pair of sunglasses as he continued to follow her.

Clarissa walked with her mind on recent events. Never in her life could she remember when just the touch of someone enticed her body's response like his. She had never been interested in men and yet, this man, this one being touched her innocently, carelessly and set her aflame. As they entered the clearing, she headed for the lake. The water shimmered in the light. She bent down and filled her canteen before she removed her backpack. She then removed her clothing to reveal a bikini underneath her garments. Diving into the water, she let the coolness disperse the heat of her physique.

Mel followed her and watched as she stripped down to the smallest excuse for a covering he had ever seen. The demon ground his teeth as he turned away from the tempting picture she made. She was nothing like he initially thought and he hated being surprised. The ability to read people had been his defense for centuries. As judge and executioner of demon kind, he never allowed himself to get close to anyone. they were a means to an end, peons to help him reach an objective. Azamel walked over to a boulder and sat down, lighting a cigarette to give his hands something to do. He opened his senses to his surroundings, trying to trace the escaped demon. Feeling Xon's essence, he sent him a mental projection. *'I am coming for you Xon. I see you, I feel you. You can try to hide but if you think that stone will protect you, you are very wrong. I will find you and I will pry it out of your dead, rotting flesh.'*

He turned his head and watched as she swam around, her body gliding through the water, a true temptress. He felt his body grow hard with desire. Getting up, thoroughly pissed at himself for allowing her even a little under his skin, Mel spoke more gruff than intended.

"We need to get going, Xon is on the move."

Clarissa looked up at him and sighed. She had needed to center herself again, yet all thoughts were how his scent invaded and enflamed her whole body. How his form felt while he protected her. He considered her a childish burden, a nuisance, yet he affected her so strongly and in ways the young wolf never imagined.

She made her way to the shore, the water dripping in soft cascades down her body. She materialized a towel and scrubbed her hair dry. "I do not care that he is on the move, you stink thanks to those Wendigos. It's an offense to my wolf sensitivities. Either clean up or head out on your own."

Ignoring him and his condescending attitude, Clarissa turned around. She grabbed her backpack, flashing on a fresh clean outfit and a comb for her hair. She then sat on the ground to comb it.

Thoroughly aggravated at her effect on him and her insults, Azamel shook with the urge to blast her. Normally he would have but he needed her to find the stone and Xon. He magically removed his clothes and stalked towards the lake, unconcerned about his nakedness. His body's reaction to the little wolf was a complication that he did not anticipate and it pissed him off. Mel dove into the cold water hoping to get some clarity. After he swam a few laps, he got out, flashed dry and into new clothing. As he walked, his weapons materialized into clips and holsters. He continued towards the path before he stopped and turned towards her. "Are you coming?"

She flashed in front of him. "As soon as you start moving your ass outta my way. Or do you plan on finding all the traps with your big feet again?"

Azamel looked her up and down with a sneer. "Since you are in front of me, I would love to know how I can be in your way. We are wasting valuable time, time that fucker will use against us. As I see it, we have three options: we can stand here, argue and sling one liners at each other or we can get moving and find that gem."

Clarissa shook her head as she spun around and started moving down the path. "That's only two. Glad to know you can count."

Azamel muttered under his breath, "That is because you really don't want to know the third." He followed quietly.

Clarissa called back, "I heard that." She knew he was behind her and his scent still played havoc with her body. To focus, she dug her nails into her palms. She needed to reach their goal. It was imperative. It was her duty, albeit one she wished she had known about, been trained for. Although she realized her mother had not thought her ready and tried to protect her childhood. *'You only get to be carefree and young once in your life. Enjoy it.'* Her family thought they had time to train and prepare her for her role as the Gem of Power's guardian. Who had ever suspected that their lives would be destroyed in one moment of horror when her entire family was killed? Who would have guessed the dagger she took to protect herself was actually a family heirloom which held her destiny? This and because she was the only female of the line who survived, the duty fell to her to become the next protector, ready or not?

As Clarissa hiked through the woods, memories flooded her as she remembered the first vision she ever had. The day she discovered that she needed to do something, even though she had no idea what that was. Alone in her apartment, she picked up the dagger and promptly collapsed on the floor, convulsing slightly while in the throes of her first trance. In the revelation, her deceased mother called her home. She dreaded going, even though she knew she had to. Painfully aware that she had put off her return and thereby facing the tragedy that had ended her peaceful existence, she made the

journey to the place of her birth. She knew she
needed to burn the dead, burn the house, salt the
earth so to speak. Her heart clenched at the
recollection, twisted agonizingly inside her chest at
the anamnesis of her family's remains, people she
spent every day of her life with until forced by her
brothers to run in order to spare her own.

When Clarissa returned to the family ranch
just outside of a small village, she fell to her knees in
despair. It was hard to see the devastation she had
left behind hurriedly. How the memories assailed her
as she walked from room to room. While shuffling
through the home another vision struck and aided
her understanding of why she had been called home.
It was much clearer. In her parent's bedroom, she
was shown the conversations that her father and
mother had about training Clarissa for her destiny.
About how she was still so young and should have
full control of her powers before they told her of her
family duty. *'If only I had overheard those
conversations. If only I had a chance to be trained
appropriately and properly. If only. If only wishes
were ponies, right?'*

It took every ounce of willpower she had to
gather the bodies of her family and say her
goodbyes. After she obtained a few personal

belongings from her childhood home, mementos of her parents, brothers and sisters, she set the building ablaze with all inside.

Unknowingly, she gasped aloud as the retrospection assailed her senses. She stopped suddenly, letting the agony wash through her. The anguish she thought was buried deep within her soul until but a moment ago.

Azamel frowned as her thoughts whispered through his mind. Suddenly, a lot of things made more sense. The responsibility she carried was heavy for someone as young as she was, yet her commitment and dedication unique for someone her age. He was so deep in thought he did not notice her stop and walked right into her. He grabbed her in his arms to keep them both from falling.

She felt his arms encircle her but the pain of her memories was great and his touch was just a reminder of what she could never have as a result of her obligation. "Sorry. Next time I will put on my brake lights." She looked around. "I thought another trap was nearby. I just wanted to get my bearings. We have a ways to go before the next one yet."

He nodded. Her agony and despair reached out to him and reluctantly Mel felt sympathy stir within his depths. Shaking his head slightly, he berated himself for daring to feel, to care. *'I am the Executioner, not some pussy to be affected by a sop story. For all I know she is aware of my ability and is using it to weaken me. Through the centuries many females have tried to tame me but this sure is rich.'*

Clarissa sighed softly and put her hand up to alert him she was about to halt again. "Trap ahead. I am not sure what the danger is. I do not know what he did, I just recognize the area."

Mel scanned the area. He felt a pulsing energy coming from the ground but could not pinpoint it. "Move slowly and keep your eyes open."

She flashed in a walking stick and used it to help guide her as she moved forward pausing in between stops. "Can't tell anything more specific, Mr. Almighty? No fixing whatever the problem is?" Her stick hit the edge of what looked like solid ground. It sank instead and she was thrown off balance.

Azamel grabbed her arm and pulled her to safety. "Quicksand." He took a small boulder and threw it on the ground about ten feet ahead of them. It was swiftly swallowed. Mel bent down and placed his hand flat on the ground. He let his powers flow into the earth, firming to form a hard crust in front of them. As he stood up, he turned to her with a frown. "You know? I get it. You are pissed at the responsibility you carry, pissed at whoever slaughtered your family, pissed at me for needing me. I get it. I have done nothing but help you but frankly I am getting fed up with your fucking attitude. You want to lash out? Lash out at the people that deserve it, not those that were not there nor had anything to do with what happened to you or your family. I never claimed to be anything I am not. You however are a fucking hypocrite. You want my help, you need my help yet you use any and all opportunities to insult me. You distrust me and belittle the effort I am making to help you. You know what? Fuck you! I have bigger demons to find and much more important things to do than put up with your fucked up issues. See you later, sweetheart!" He stalked off.

She stood still as he stormed away. Astounded at his words, Clarissa almost felt violated that he knew so much about her. She had been snarky towards him but that was her defense. He managed to get under her skin and she could not have that, no matter how delectable he looked or how his touch set her body on fire. She slowly followed him, keeping a good distance back. The guardian was unaware of any other traps and they needed to get to the stone before the demon did.

Rage clouded his vision but he kept walking until a faint sound behind him reached his ears. Against his better judgment he stopped and turned around. The gem called out, rang in her head, alarms that screeched, whined and forced her to her knees. She held her hands over her ears even though the sound was strictly internal, whimpering from the pain. Blinding light flashed between her eyes and Clarissa knew she failed her duty. Mel rushed over and knelt beside her, his anger momentarily forgotten. He took her head between his hands and forced her to look at him. Flashing his glasses away he spoke in a harsh tone, "Clarissa! Look at me! Look! Focus on me! Breathe through it!"

She felt hands on her, pulling her, loud words that did not make sense. Her cheeks were slowly becoming wet with tears of pain. She moaned a bit more but then noticed a pair of light baby blue eyes that seemed to pierce her soul and break through the sounds that reverberated within her skull. His words were finally becoming clear and her breathing settled as the cacophony slowly died. She focused on him, getting lost in his eyes as her breathing remained slightly ragged but for entirely different reasons. After a moment or two, she cleared her throat lightly. "Am. Okay. I think. He has the hidden part of the stone. You were right. I have failed."

Azamel lifted her chin, a feeling of awkwardness surround them. "Xon found it. he won the battle but not the war. Look at me! He still needs the other part. That means he will be coming to find you. He will be exposed and we will get it back. When he surfaces, he will die." Mel used his thumbs to gently wipe the tears off her cheek.

"How do you know so much about the stone? Only a small few know it is in more than one piece." Her wet lashes caressed her cheeks as she blinked, her breath caught with his tenderness. Again she got lost in those baby blues.

Azamel mentally cursed himself for letting that slip. His mind scrambled as he tried to think of a suitable reply that would placate her and repair the fragile trust they had between them. Thinking that this was probably the stupidest thing he had ever done in his endlessly long life, he leaned forward and took her mouth in a hard kiss. The intention was to distract her from her train of thought. However, the moment their lips met, everything changed. Her soft sigh as he pressed his tongue against hers jolted his body and mind. Keeping his hands in her hair, he deepened the kiss feasting on her soft mouth with a hunger that burned through his entire being.

He tasted as divine as she had tried so desperately to not imagine. His scent lifted her to the heights of intoxication. She found herself breathless in milliseconds from his passionate hunger. It seemed to call out to her with as much desire as hers wanted to respond to. She could feel all her womanly parts tingle in response to his closeness as she was lost in the moment. She did not care if he was using her or not to gain the stone for himself. Right now, she wanted this point in time to last, although she knew it was impossible and yet he held her so tight she could not break free, even if she wanted to.

Clarissa's response fueled Mel's desire and heated his blood. However, it also shocked him to his very core. With a deep growl, the executioner pulled his lips away from hers and stood up, moving quickly a few feet away. His breathing was harsh as he shoved his shaking hands through his hair. Mel flashed his glasses back on and made a show of picking up the backpack. "I," he cleared his throat trying to regain some semblance of control. "I think we need to head back."

Her voice was still tight with desire as she talked. "Head back?" *Why can I not think? Concentrate. What did he say?* "I have to find Xon. I have to get the stone back." The guardian climbed shakily to her feet and readjusted the backpack on her shoulders after taking it from him. She wanted to bring the dagger out and try to get a reading. In truth, she could not contemplate the energy she needed to activate her visions with the pangs of pain and passion that so recently coursed through her body. Turning, Clarissa retraced her steps back down the path, silent, thinking, trying to understand what she was feeling and how it fit into her duties as the gems custodian.

He whirled on her and grabbed her arms, shaking her slightly as fury coated his baritone voice. "Where will you look for him? Are you going to try and trace him? Then what? You knock yourself out from the effort? You know he will come for it. Rather than chase him, let Xon come to us. We can lure him out. We can set the scene as we want it. You need to fight him in familiar territory, which gives you the upper hand. Come on." Mel gently pulled her along. "You need to rest. You will be of no use to yourself or anyone else if you are worn out."

Clarissa followed along meekly, her free hand going slightly to her lips when he was not looking. She still felt the ghost pressure against her skin, felt his mouth as it took possession, his tongue against hers, his taste still invaded her senses. Snarling slightly to herself, she dropped her fingers away from her lips angrily. *'Yeah! This is just what I need to do! I should waste time on a fantasy of being with this arrogant man? I have a duty to perform not play at schoolgirl crushes.'* She wanted to pull her fingers away from his but she knew that would only make him aware of how he affected her and she was not about to do that. *'Stone. Stone. I have a duty. I have a responsibility to the Gem of Power. Think of only that. That is my only obligation. Concentrate!'*

She finally spoke, her words were harsher than she meant for them to be. "Mind telling me how we do this? What familiar territory?" She managed to finally pull her hand from his grasp, though more for her own sanity than anything else. The custodian for the gem folded her arms to hide their slight shaking. She stood with her legs askew to maintain her own weak balance. "I would prefer going to him and getting the upper hand in a surprise attack."

Mel snarled. "If you think for one minute that Xon will not expect you to come for him immediately, you are deluding yourself. He will draw you in and arrange it so you will not only relinquish the other part but will probably lose your life in the process. I am not about to let that happen. He cannot be allowed access to the powers that the gem offers and I will not permit him to take your life. If we set up the scene and let him know we have it and where, subtly of course, he will come to us. We will wait, gain the upper advantage because he will be eager, anxious and that will cause him to make stupid mistakes."

Clarissa sighed as she bit her lower lip and cast her eyes downward. "In truth I am not sure what to do. I am not a strategist. I had hoped to gain the hidden portion of the gem before he reached it." She looked up, her eyes softer as they gazed at him.

Azamel gave her a wicked smile. "I am an excellent tactician and at this point you will be safest with me until we are ready to confront him. He cannot touch me nor enter my home as it is in a realm he does not have access to. I suggest we go there where we will be off the grid to him. The frustration will drive Xon to expose himself."

The guardian could not help but start to tease him just a little. "Oh? Come over to your place?" Clarissa raised an eyebrow and scowled. She surprised herself with the harshness of the words that followed. "Really? What kind of a girl do you think I am? Wanna try and get me drunk too?" She had to wonder if she pissed him off even more than she had since she met him. *'Damn it! Why did I have to say that? Why am I so caustic with him.'* Then realization dawned upon her. She knew instantly why she was so astringent toward Azamel. He scared her. The emotions he raised within her made her nervous because she did not want to get involved with anyone, much less someone who would not and could not be a part of her life. It was just another person the custodian would lose and she had lost so many so much already. She turned away from him so he would not see the truth behind her feelings.

Mel squeezed his eyes shut to control the anger that boiled within him as a result of her words. He sensed the warring emotions inside her. Now was not the time, however, to delve into the internal turmoil that she felt. It was also not the time to explore the protectiveness and frustrations that she stirred in him. Her fighting spirit and the deeply buried hurt inside her awakened affectionate warmth inside his cold, dead heart. It scared him to his very core. This *girl* affected him like no other and he absolutely detested that fact. He felt like he hated her for it. He wanted to lash out and hurt her, punish her for making him care about another, to be concerned if another lived or died. He had never attached himself to anyone for he was meant to walk alone for eternity. He was required to rid the earth from those who set out to hurt it and its inhabitants. He glared at her. His eyes the color of blood, visible even through the glasses he wore as the demon part of him threatened to rise up from within.

Clarissa took a deep breath to calm her shaking nerves. "I am sorry. I should not have said that. You are, of course correct. I am sure you are a wonderful strategist and I bow to your expertise as well as thank you for your offer of assistance."

Her apology helped to calm Mel's inner beast and send the creature back to a forced slumber within him. Once the demon was settled, the executioner held his fingers out to her. "I need you to take my hand. We don't have much time before Xon will catch your essence and come here. We are not prepared for him and must retreat until such time as we can successfully engage him."

Clarissa turned to him with a stoicism she barely felt registering on her face. She looked at his outstretched hand. After hesitating slightly, she placed her fingers softly against his. She trusted him and that was very hard for her to do. This woman had trusted no one since her family had been slaughtered in front of her. But Clarissa was desperate to get the stone back and she realized she could not do it alone.

Azamel wanted to help her, whether for his own selfish needs of trying to obtain the Gem of Power with the gifts it offered for himself or because he really was devoted to containing the demons that were under his jurisdiction. Either way, she knew he was an extremely old creature and they said with age came wisdom. Maybe she would learn some knowledge from him and be able to protect the stone better. Everything else, this receptivity he brought out in her, feelings of desire and concern for him were something she was going to have to ignore in order to do her duty. Her life was all about obligation and she handled the responsibility as efficiently as possible, regardless of the sacrifices she had to make in the process. Clasping her hand lightly to his, she nodded firmly once.

Mel looked down at their joined hands and lightly rubbed his thumb over her knuckles. Her face showed raw determination as the executioner teleported them both to his home. A fire already crackled in the hearth and a pleasant warmth embraced them. He let go of her hand after giving it a reassuring squeeze.

"Welcome to my abode, little one." He gestured to the couch in front of the fire. "Please, make yourself at home. If you would excuse me, I will be but a moment." Azamel inclined his head towards her before he willed himself to his private chambers, leaving her alone momentarily.

Grateful to be in the privacy of his room, Mel flashed his clothes away and padded to the bathroom. He welcomed the warmth of the spray as he stepped into the shower. His mind reeled as he leaned his head back and let the water hit his face before the beads cascaded down his body and over his taut muscles. Refreshed and feeling more in control, he rubbed himself dry, the friction ridding him of all vestiges of the battle they fought as well as helped him to regain some semblance of control over his wayward and conflicted emotions.

As soon as he disappeared, Clarissa let out a breath she had not realized she was holding. She took a moment to look around. The room seemed to be pretty isolated with no windows and one door. There was a long wooden table with eight lavish red and gold chairs. In front of the fireplace, there were two wing-backed blue chairs and a matching blue couch on the opposite side. What disturbed her the most however, were the winged gargoyle skeletons that flanked either side of the fireplace mantle holding scones that provided the light for the area.

Since Mel seemed intent on leaving her alone for the moment, she allowed the remnants of the pain in her head followed by his kiss which had left her off-guard, unsure, to be investigated more thoroughly. She did not particularly care for those feelings brought about by his closeness.

Taking a cleansing breath, the guardian was uncertain if she was being watched or not. If she was, Clarissa was unaware of who might be spying on her. However, she had to take the chance and see whatever the dagger would show her, if anything. The guardian needed guidance and she knew the gem only had one motive, keeping the rest of the stone safe. Pulling her backpack off, she laid it by her feet and sat on the couch. Looking around again, feeling a bit safe, she brought forth the power's receptacle to focus on where the demon named Xon was and what he might be up to.

As Clarissa clutched the dagger and concentrated, Mel's abode melted away. It blended into a solid darkness, which then started to become dim outlines of a lush jungle. Dense green, the smell of the wooded pines and oaks permeated her nose. She heard the sounds of pounding feet rustling through the leaves and brush. Muttering soon came into focus as did the demon himself. Xon could not understand why the stone did not work. He wanted to make a camp and examine his prize, try to figure it out.

The vision then turned to Azamel and her in the jungle as they searched for Xon. She saw him holding her as he tried to get her to focus while she knelt in pain. The past events rolled by as if on a movie screen within her mind. She watched as she surprised him with her question and he looked like he was caught with his hand in the cookie jar. He leaned forward to kiss her. She still remembered what that felt like. However, now she saw it with dispassionate eyes, saw him using that kiss like a ploy, to distract her and it worked. Her vision cleared.

'Gods I am gullible! How he must be laughing at me even now.'

She put the dagger away as she berated herself for being so stupid, so simplistic. After everything she had been though, knowing she should not trust anyone, she let one kiss from some hot, stubborn man spin her world around so she saw nothing other than him. Mel was using her. He knew all about the stone and he was manipulating her to get it. She had been foolish enough to let him, blinded by her own stupid feelings. *'Some guardian I made!'* She starred into the fire, trying to decide what to do.

Chapter Three

Dressed in all black attire, he materialized behind her. Mel silently watched as she sat on the couch. She was a stranger in his otherwise almost unoccupied dwelling. Softly, so as not to startle her, Azamel spoke. "Is there anything you need? Would you like food or something to drink? I will have my servant, Shara show you to your chambers as soon as they are ready."

His scent reached her nose before his voice reached her ears. At the mention of food she realized with the exception of water, she had ingested nothing for over twenty four hours. She should be famished but everything she learned made her too upset to eat. Turning her head back to the fire, unable to look at him knowing what she now knew. "I am fine."

Mel frowned at her sudden cold demeanor, not sure what brought it on. Gently probing so to not alert her to the extent of his powers, Azamel realized she was starving yet she refused any sustenance. He waved his hand and the table became laden with delicious dishes which appeared in front of them. "We might be here a while and you need to keep your strength up. Please join me?"

Clarissa concentrated on the fire, knowing if she looked at him or the sustenance he provided, she would lose all resolve. The smell of the food already enticed her as her stomach betrayed her by growling in anticipation of eating. "How long do you think I will be," She thought *stuck* but said, "here?"

"You are not a prisoner. I only asked you here for your own protection. Xon would not dare come to my home and that will give us time to plan without concern for your safety." He stood very still, watched her intently as he took a plate and held in towards her.

She knew how powerful he was and wondered if he could read her thoughts or just heard the sound of her body as it grumbled emptily again. Clarissa kept her mind purposefully blank. Her mental shields, although weak, were up just in case. She still had so much to learn that her family never got the chance to teach her, like this destiny she was now burdened with and failing miserably at. Still, if she were pleasant but watchful, she might be able to use Azamel instead. She knew what he wanted from her now so if she enticed him and was friendly then maybe she would be able to keep him thrown off-guard. Maybe she would succeed in getting the stone returned to her trust while at the same time also prevent Mel from acquiring it. *'Just think with your head and not your hormones,'* she told herself and turne d to finally face him as she gave a slight incline of her head as she took the plate from his hands. "Thank you."

He nodded as he moved to sit at the table, watching her carefully. "You managed to trace the demon and knew where all the traps were set. How did you obtain that information?"

Clarissa shrugged as she put some food on the plate. "I just did. How did you find me? Know about me? How did you know the stone was in more than one piece?" She turned a stoic look to him. "You seem to know a lot, want to tell me about it?"

Mel chuckled. "Now, now love. I asked you first. Besides you forget that I not only live with demons, rule demons but I also am one."

"I cannot forget something I did not know. Maybe you should tell me more about yourself and I might possibly consider answering your questions."

"You should know better than to play that game with me. I thought we moved past this in the jungle? I want to know how to help you. Me and my background have no relevance to this and trust me you really do not want to know. There is only one person that knows everything about me and you are looking at him." He leaned forward. "You and I both know I do not need to ask you. I can take the information from you without your knowing. I gave you my word that I would help you and that includes not violating your thoughts. Now, can we try this again?"

"Why should I tell you all my secrets if you're not going to share? Do you not think that is a bit one sided. If you want to," Tried to think of a word that might irk him. "Rape my mind and steal my secrets, I am not going to be able to stop you. I know you're far more powerful than me. I can sense that much of you. Therefore, I am sure I will be unable to do anything to prevent you from forcibly taking from my mind anything you wish to know."

Clarissa stood holding the plate with both hands so the shaking she was inwardly feeling would not show. She stood with her chin raised, proud, stubborn and defiant. "The fact that you chose not to have done so yet is gallant, to say the least. But you might wish to remember you came to me. I did not seek out you or your assistance. Although, I appreciate your offer, your motives concern me. As for moving past this in the jungle, the goal was different then. You deal with the demon, I deal with the stone, both happy and both move our separate ways. I failed in getting to the stone first. You offered strategy where I know none. I accepted. But if it is contingent on my telling you about me or the stone then the price for your guidance is too high."

The guardian wondered what his next move would be. Will he relinquish information for a chance at the stone or just push her away? Her heart beat rapidly as she looked at this sexy man, wanting the help but not willing to show weakness. *'Gods give me the strength I need to resist him and focus on my duties.'*

"The goal has not changed and I will not violate your mind. I made a promise and my word is my honor." He turned away from her and towards the fire, his hands clasped behind his back. "You are young and your powers are still growing. I was only suggesting you tell me since I may be able to help you either develop them or add some of mine to help you find Xon easier." He turned back to face her. "Trust is as hard for me as it is for you."

His words shocked her so much she dropped the plate. The little bit of food she had placed on it scattered across the floor. Her mouth went dry, her mind raced. He was someone willing to teach her? Help her? Someone who can add power to her abilities? She did not know what to say. Yet she felt there was an underlying ambition to his offer of assistance like the Gem of Power. Still as promised, he had fought by her side. He had even saved her life. He knew about her but not enough to decipher what powers she controlled. Mel could tell they were raw but then anyone who knew anything about weres knew the young ones were still learning. By were standards, she was still very young in her power abilities.

"Answer the question of how you know the stone is in more than one piece. Please."

She stood ramrod still though she was a bowl of jelly inside, nervous and worried of what his reply would be or even if he would answer.

"Honestly, I did not know the stone was in more than one piece. I felt the demon and his lust for power. Believe me, he is the last one you would want as keeper of that gem. He is only after the power it will enable him with and has no concern of who he may hurt in the process. That means you too. I assumed something was amiss when he got the stone and nothing had happened."

"That makes sense." Clarissa thought about his explanation. It certainly was logical enough. In all fairness she answered one of his questions.

"Psychometry is the official name for the power that allowed me to gain the knowledge of the traps he set, though most would call it premonitions. However, I also see past and future events as well when I hold or touch a person or object." She used her telekinesis to clean up the mess she made and then held it in the air around her. The guardian appea red to be the center of the universe with the planets orbiting about them only it was pieces of food and bits of broken plate suspended instead. "Garbage?"

Mel waved a hand and all the pieces vanished.

"Garbage. Now eat please. If you want me to teach you, I will need you at full strength and fully rested. I will warn you, training with me will not be easy."

Clarissa gathered another plate and concentrated on the food laden table. "What do you get out of this? Helping me, teaching me I mean."

"I get to keep a demon from having one of the most powerful tools known to our kind, how much more noble do I need to be?" He sat down at the table across from her.

She tilted head and could not resist looking at him. "You do not need to teach me nobility."

"I know." He took a sip from the goblet in front of him, watching as she ate. Mel wondered what it was about her that drew him. She was beautiful but he had been around beautiful women before. Azamel cocked his head slightly, his gaze still unreadable. She had a fiery spirit and determination that was like a magnet to him. The way she lifted her chin, her passionate resolve to protect those near her, she intrigued yet scared him. She concerned him but still enticed him to help her, to be around her.

"Let's just say I don't like to see an innocent harmed."

His face was shadowed and blank as if he were trying to figure out something as he surveyed her. She in turn watched him questioningly. He admitted he was a demon and yet she found herself drawn to him. A creature she should have not and in fact, does not have any reason to trust, yet something about him compelled her to want to confide in him, believe in him. She had to remember that her visions were never one hundred percent accurate due to interpretation. The perception of them together could be completely off base and she would end up dead at his feet regardless of what she saw in her mind's eye. However, she knew he wanted the stone. She nibbled at a strawberry while she continued to think. If the custodian knew the ultimate goal of his was the gem, she can maybe blind-side him when it came down to the final moment between them. Maybe if he got to know her, he would show some true compassion to all that he had been pretending and let her hide the powerful object safely away again.

Becoming resolved, she decided to try a little kindness. Her mother always told her, "You attract the bees more with honey than with vinegar." Maybe her mother had a valid point. "Nice place. Lived here long?"

Mel smiled at her obvious ploy at changing the topic.

"Longer than you will know, love. Is there anything you need? I can have your things brought here if you desire."

He focused on his drink so as not to look at her, all vulnerable and still looking defiant as if she dared him to abuse her in any way. She had spirit and it drew him to her like a moth to a flame. He thought back on how her lips felt under his and he had to close his eyes for a moment to banish the image and the feelings that stirred within him. But that only made the memory more vibrant. Once he opened his pale blue orbs, he could not seem to focus beyond her lips and the way her teeth nibbled on the ripe fruit in her hand.

"If all your answers are going to be so vague, should I continue asking questions?" She took another bite of strawberry, her lips molded around the red juicy fruit before she bit down on it. "Are you not eating? Or does your fare consist of only what you drink?"

Azamel gave a tiny shake of his head to clear the image from his mind. "Believe me, love, pray you never find out what I eat." He rolled the stem of the goblet in his hands. "You seem to have ignored one of my questions. If you don't need anything from home and would rather prefer to walk around naked, who am I to complain?" He gave her a charming smile and a slow, hot once over.

His look sent shivers down to her toes and made her stomach clench with desire. "A room with a hot shower would be nice. I think I can handle my own change of clothes without running around your abode naked despite how exciting that would be for you." She put a bit more food on her plate, picked at the chicken with her fingers before putting them in her mouth, slightly sucking on them. "You said you would train me. Should we begin after my shower?"

He felt his throat constrict gazing at her. What she was doing to the food was cruel and enticing his body to respond in a way he had no desire for it to. Needing the space, he stood up and shoved the chair back harshly. "Finish your meal while I see to the room. We can start after you are settled." He stalked down the corridor, his hands in his pockets while trying to stop the slight tremble they seemed insistent on doing.

She jumped slightly at the scrape of chair and her eyes followed him as he stormed off wondering what she said or did to upset him this time. And she did it without even trying. Scooping up one more spoonful that she polished it off quickly, Clarissa made her way once again to the hearth. The fire sent warmth to her chilled bones but the heat did not seep in. It was probably because the chill was not caused by anything exterior. In her mind's eye she saw her home on fire, stared as it burned to the ground, along with it all the memories and dreams, happy and otherwise that she had. She realized right then how scared and solitary she was. Clarissa pretended it did not matter, that she did not care and her obligations and responsibilities were all that concerned her now. But in truth, she missed her family and her friends terribly. She felt alone and hated it.

Mel made sure her suite was comfortable and ready. He sauntered back to the hall, knowing that his servant, Shara could have done what he just did but he needed the space to clear his head. As he entered the room, the executioner saw the guardian in front of the mantle. She looked lost and forlorn and it tugged at a heart that he had thought dead for a millennia. What was it about her that made his body respond in ways he never thought possible? He stood and watched her a moment longer then cleared his throat so she would know he was there.

"Your room is ready, if you will follow me?"

Clarissa looked up, her eyes riddled with sadness

she gave one nod and moved to follow him.

Azamel looked away quickly so as not be affected by the grief in her eyes. He moved down the hall and approached a large, intricately carved door. The door magically opened silently as they approached, revealing a spacious, opulent room. A fire in the hearth warmed the interior as candlelight provided a soft, welcoming glow. Again Mel cleared his throat and stepped to the side making way for Clarissa to enter the chamber.

"There is an in-suite bathroom where, I am sure, you will find everything you need."

He felt a bit awkward and started to turn away before he stopped himself. "I, er, will be waiting for you in the great hall when you are ready."

Clarissa nodded once then spoke, her voice soft, haunted. "I won't be long. Thank you."

She unslung her backpack and undid her ponytail, letting her hair cascade about her shoulders. She spun to him, the glow behind her giving her an almost angelic halo.

"Mel? Can you tell where Xon is? How do you plan to entice him to come to us?"

Azamel took a step back towards the room. "You freshen up and we can brainstorm when you are finished."

He inclined his head and turned towards the great hall as he shut the door behind him, leaning against it for a brief moment to steady his suddenly erratic breathing.

Once he had shut the door, Clarissa took her clothes off, padded to the bathroom and turned the water on. Stepping inside, she let the water cascade over her body in rivets that coursed its way over her feminine curves. Sighing at the release of tension in her muscles as the water softly pelted her, she tilted her head back washing and rinsing her hair and loved the fact she no longer smelled like the jungle. She knew she was in there for a while but the heat and the pressure relieved her of a multitude of sweat, smells, worries, concerns and overall tension.

Finally she shut the water off and stepped out. She immediately found a couple of towels. She wrapped her hair up in one and dried herself off with the other. Flashing on a fresh pair of black skin tight jeans and a mid-rift t-shirt, she combed her hair out and made her way back into the room. She felt a hundred percent better, refreshed, until shock set in when she noticed that her backpack was opened and the contents scattered about the bed.

The guardian's heart raced as panic set in. Mel betrayed her after all! Furious and with determination, Clarissa ran to the great hall, only to stop just outside of it as she heard a conversation and wanted to listen in. A woman with a melodious voice spoke and she wondered if that was Shara whom he had mentioned earlier.

"My Lord?" Shara stood to the side of Mel with her head down she waited respectfully for him to acknowledge her. He had been acting strangely since he brought the were-wolf here. The female's presence seemed to upset and agitate him and Shara would not allow her boss to be hurt in any way. He would never know this but she cared for him deeply and mistrusted anyone who attempted to get near to him.

Hearing Shara's soft voice, he looked up to see her standing as still as a statue by him. "What is it Shara? I told you I don't want to see anybody today. I told you I do not wish to be disturbed."

"I know, my Lord, but I have something to show you and I fear it cannot wait. I. I do not trust the were-wolf you brought here and I wanted to make sure she is not here to harm you. I searched her bag and-"

Mel spun on her. "You *what*?" his voice traveled down the halls, permeated throughout his home with his anger.

Shara jumped as his rage exploded. She quickly produced the dagger and thrust it towards him. "I found this!" her voice quivered. "It was in her bag and it is not of human make. I fear she is here to assassinate you! I- I- I was only trying to protect you."

The executioner quickly glanced at the dagger then stared into the fire, his hands clenched at his sides, trying not to strangle her. After several moments, he spoke in a very low, dangerous voice. "You will return that to her immediately or so help me, Shara, your centuries of service will turn into an eternity of hell and misery in my dungeon."

Clarissa stood silently in the back, hidden in the shadows as she watched all that transpired. She was turning out to be a horrible guardian to have lost both halves of the powerful relic. Then she heard him order Shara to return it to her and she sighed softly, letting out a breath she had not realized she was holding.

Stepping forward, she held out her hand. "I will take it now."

Shara quickly moved and placed it in her open palm before she darted just as fast out of the room and left the two of them alone. Clarissa looked at Azamel, watched him closely before she spoke, "I know you know what this is. You could have kept it. Why?"

Mel shrugged noncommittally. "It was not mine to take. You are a guest in my home and I will not violate your privacy." He growled as he glowered at Shara's retreating form. "Nor will I allow it to be violated by anybody!"

That impressed her. He could take full advantage of her within his own realm. She knew he could just remove anything from her, keep it and she would be lost to it or die trying to get it back. Instead, he really did have honor and she was suddenly willing to trust him. She approached him, the dagger gripped tightly in her hand. Clarissa stood before him and held the dagger so he could see it better.

"It has part of the stone in it as you already now know. It's how I know the stone is in danger and by whom. It let me see what traps Xon set through my psychrometry." She looked up at him innocently, hopeful that he would understand what she had done for him just now.

Mel bent over the weapon slightly and examined the dagger. His eyes absorbed every carving, every dip and curve in the intricately cut metal. The stone seemed alive, pulsed with energy, called to him. He straightened and held out a hand. "May I?"

Her heart lurched again, questioned his motive, questioned if she was doing the right thing. But despite the inner turmoil and hesitancy, the custodian placed it in his palm. She stepped back, waited to see what he would do.

'Gods.' She silently prayed. *'Let me be doing the right thing in trusting him. Please Mel, do not betray me. I could not bear it.'*

Despite his actions with Shara, a part of her was still scared he would misplace her belief in him. She watched, prepared to fight to get take the relic back if necessary. Her stance slightly anticipated for fast movement as she gnawed slightly at the inside of her bottom lip, nervous that he would keep the dagger and yet scared that he would not. If he returned it then she was correct in her credence of his sincerity.

As Azamel grasped the dagger, he closed his

eyes and ran his hand over every carving, like a lover's caress. He reached out with his powers, tried to sense the energy within. Not being the guardian and the stone not being whole, he could not access any of the abilities and found it frustrating. The metal felt alive under his touch, yet nothing else came through. He opened his blue orbs, gave it another look of scrutiny and he handed it back to her handle first. "Thank you."

Clarissa took the dagger from him, sheathed it quickly then wrapped it up. She stuck it in the backpack which she had dragged with her to complain about being violated and her property stolen. She looked up at him, her eyes soft, searching. He was nothing like she expected. What she had come to anticipate from others who even knew about the stone, much less touched a part of it. She tucked a still damp curl behind her ear as she stood back up to meet him eye to eye.

"I know what you were trying to do. Read the dagger I mean. Did you see anything? See him?"

"Nothing, then again, I am not surprised. I am not guardian of the gem. I didn't really expect it to work. I might be able to help you though."

"Do you think my psychometry came from being

guardian? The psychometry really kicked in after my family," her voice cracked slightly and she paused to swallow past the lump before she continued in a strong voice, "When the responsibility fell to me."

Mel cocked his head slightly, her pain reached out to him. He fought the urge to comfort her and focused on the business at hand. "Probably yes. Your powers are strong but you need guidance. Right now, we have no time to thoroughly train you. I have a suggestion though and it may just work." He gave her a serious look. "It will not be pleasant for you."

She frowned. "Not crazy about the not pleasant part. What are you suggesting and how unpleasant?"

"You have to try to read the stone. I will boost your powers by adding some of mine but since your powers are new and virtually untapped it may be painful for you. It may be very painful."

Clarissa thought about it and moved away slightly, starring into the fire. She had tried erudition a couple of times already. What it showed her was indistinct. What came out clearly though was first the premonition of Azamel's kiss and then the reminder of it. Maybe if her powers were more focused she could get past that point of his lips on hers and do the job she was meant to do, protect the

Gem of Power. After several quiet, heavily spaced moments, she pulled out the knife unwrapping it. "Let's do this then."

He gently pulled her towards the couch and sat next to her. "Try to perceive what the stone has to relate."

Clarissa took a deep breath, closed her eyes and concentrated on calling up the power she would need for her visions. At first nothing happened then her eyes glossed over under the closed lids and she started to convulse. She slipped into the realm of her premonitions. They were still slightly unclear. She envisioned lush brush that Xon clomped over or moved aside. The shrubs were too heavily thick to see clearly where he was or her powers were just not strong enough to see past them and get a better reading. Was he still near the cave where the other half had been buried? Did he sense that the stone bearing dagger had been there? Was he even now searching for it?

Mel watched the guardian go into a trance, the dagger rested lightly in her palms. He moved his hands under hers, his palms placed on the backs of her hands. She gave a very slight start as his skin touched hers but she did not move away. He closed his eyes and let his force flow into her, his extremities warming hers. She jerked slightly from the intrusion but soon settled. Gradually Mel increased the power he sent into her body.

Clarissa felt the jolt of electricity pierce her being. With his abilities boosting hers, she was able to have the vision of Xon clear. She saw him now, not from his eyes but from the area. The stone was in a pouch he wore around his bulging neck. His eyes yellow gleamed trying to pick up the sense of the other half of the gem needed to make it work. Xon took it out and held it for a few moments, used it as a dousing rod trying to discern the other half's current location but it only took him to the places Mel and her had been.

The paths where they argued and managed his traps, which by the way, he seemed none too pleased with that they were dismantled. The relic guided Xon to the lake where they cleaned up a bit and she saw Mel naked. To the area that still held the knee imprints of her collapsing in pain from the stone being taken into another's grasp. Xon was frustrated the guardian could feel it but Xon's bellow of rage confirmed it.

The piece he had was telling him nothing of

where the other section was that he needed to make it whole. He swung and ripped out the trees, setting them on fire with a thought, furious at the fact the stone would not work for him. Xon's fury pierced Clarissa's brain and she softly whimpered.

Azamel heard the soft cry from her, removed his hands and therefore his extra push of power. Breaking away so suddenly was like tearing a piece of her soul and she howled out painfully. Her body convulsed wildly and she dropped the dagger as the burning, piercing sensation wracked every molecule within her. She stopped shaking and toppled over unconscious. The pain took its toll on her, ripped her insides apart in such a way that passing out was the only thing left her body could do.

"Fuck!" he cursed loudly and fell on his knees next to her unconscious form. He lifted her head, his fingers at her throat. Relieved as he felt a strong pulse, he carefully picked her up and carried her to the quarters he had given her. He laid her down gently on the huge bed as he lifted his hands and moved them over her body. The warmth emanating from them relaxed her and soothed the pain. Mel moved back and took a seat in the armchair next to the bed as he waited for her to become conscious once again.

Lost to the peaceful darkness, the pain pulled away from her, Clarissa was content to remain where she was, in blissful obscurity. No pain, no feelings of loss, no duties that she had to attend to. Nothingness enveloped around her and she let it, sank into it, giving herself over to the quietness. The tranquility called to her and she was content to remain in the idyllic surrounding, letting a euphoric feeling encompass her. Her exterior body remained still on the bed, her breathing even but shallow, lost to unconsciousness.

Her breathing slowed, she was calmer and her face was more relaxed. Mel used the opportunity to study her features. The strength inside her was palpable even in rest. He resisted the urge to probe inside her mind, not wanting to disturb her peaceful countenance yet he realized they had very limited time to secure the stone.

A conscience he did not think he had was speaking to him. *'I want that stone, for centuries I thought it lost to me. Its power lures me even now, yet something is holding me back, preventing me from taking it as I always do when I yearn for something. I seek what I crave and I take it, yet I suddenly find myself in a precarious position. That which I long for is not necessarily that which I desired when I started this journey.'*

The warring emotions within the executioner were both frightening and exhilarating. Unsure as to how to proceed, Mel stood up and walked to the door. He stopped, not being able to resist a last look at her. As he turned his head, he found her emerald green eyes upon him.

She had sensed his retreating presence and it pulled her out of her dark security, allowed duty and feeling to return. She watched his backside as he made his way to the door, surprised when he turned and she found herself starring into those pale baby blues once again. They were the color of the sky on an approaching storm, the peace just before the torrent rage of wind and rain. She gazed at him. A part of her did not want him to go, another needed to end this mission quickly and successfully before all of her was lost to him.

"Xon is very angry because he does not know where the stone went."

Azamel was glad that she spoke and broke the awkward atmosphere that settled in the room. "How do you feel?" Immediately he felt stupid for even asking. He cleared his throat and continued a bit more gruffly, "You just fainted on me. I was not sure if my powers did that or it was the result of something else."

Clarissa sat up and lowered her head. "Painful was an understatement on the warning. I sensed your power and I saw the demon better, felt him actually. Could feel the rage he had that he was not succeeding and it was taking longer than he estimated. I felt you pull back and it was like you were pulling me apart with the power you were withdrawing." She raised her legs on the bed and wrapped her arms about them, huddled within herself as she tried to overcome the memory of it, almost still feeling the tentacles of pain that coursed through her.

"It was like you were pulling my essence? My soul even?" She shook her head. "Something that was me out of me."

Azamel put his hands in his pockets to give them a place to be but also to stop him from doing something stupid, like take her in his arms and comfort her. He took a very nonchalant pose, hoping she bought the air of indifference he liked to keep around him. "That is one of the aspects of your powers that you need to learn. It is also the most dangerous. When your essence separates from your physical body, your body is vulnerable until your entity returns. You will need to make sure you are in a safe place. Sometimes the pain is almost unbearable."

Clarissa peered up at him, with an almost a pitiful look. "It never hurt like that, ever. A friend told me I convulsively shake and that my eyes gloss over. It comes over me sometimes with other things or even people." She thought about the first time she touched him but said nothing about that as she continued, "With the dagger, however it comes usually whenever I concentrate. It never hurt before. Nothing like that had ever happened previously."

"I wish I could tell you that it would not be painful but that would be giving you false expectations. I only shared some of my powers with you, the ones you needed to strengthen your own. That was a mere pittance of the abilities that you could have or the ones that you will need to cope with. It will take practice and time which we don't have. I-" he spoke through gritted teeth, the thought of being close to her both excited and scared him. "I can teach you, help you build your strength."

She heard the gruff tone and stood up, anger infused her. "Oh please! Do not bother! I would hate to be more of a burden to you than I already am. Obviously I have taken up a lot of your precious time as is." She lifted her chin defiantly. "Your demon friend is looking for me. Let me out of here and I will go deal with him and then you never have to see me again. I won't be this hindrance on you any longer!"

Before she had a chance to blink Mel had her by the throat, her toes dangled a foot above the ground. His eyes flashed red and the demon inside of him reared its head for a split second before he masked it. She caught a glimpse of his evil side as her eyes widen. Mel's voice was so low it was almost demonic, "*Do not push me*! You have no idea who you are dealing with and what I can do to you. The loss of your family will be but a flutter compared to the eternal pain and anguish I am capable of giving you. I am helping you out of my own free will, out of a noble wish to not let evil roam freely. Do not ever try that with me again."

Her eyes widened and then narrowed. Her hands clamped around his still around her throat, cutting off her air supply slightly. There was a part of her that just willed him to take her life and get it over with. The fact he knew about her family, about her heartache infuriated her further.

She kneed him so hard, she was sure he would never increase the spawn of his existence by creating off-spring. His grip lessened for a moment. She was not sure if it was out of surprise that she would dare such a thing or if she really did hurt him. With were-wolf speed, his hands still encircled by hers, she twisted and flipped him over her shoulder onto the floor before he even had a chance to blink. She straddled him and pinned his arms down, using his weight against him. Growling, low and deep, inhuman, she snarled. "Your offer to," She spat out the next word, "help was offered with disdain. You wanna kill me, do it. You think I am scared of the anguish as a result of the loss of my family that you know nothing about then you're wrong. *Anything* is bliss compared to what I live through on a daily basis."

His eyes became a deeper red then she ever saw before, something she did not think possible. Her heart raced with fear but she would not give in to it, she would not give in to him. He was momentarily winded and just stared up at her. *'Fuck me, I forgot how strong a were can be.'* He twisted his body around, let her fall on her back then pinned her with his body. She squirmed but she could not move other than growl insults at him. Her eyes were flashing, the anger and aggression bled from her.

"Will you stop? How is this helping? I am getting up now. If you still want to leave then go, find him yourself, get killed, that makes no difference to me, sweetheart. You think I care about your death? You know nothing." He tried desperately not to think about how soft her body was beneath his and the way his traitorous body was responding to her.

All of her despair and hatred for living when everyone was gone just poured through every pore of her body. She squirmed as she tried to fight him, attempted to get him off of her and became more frustrated when she could not.

"You started this! Why should you care anything about me, much less my death?"

She managed to free an arm and beat upon his chest, trying to dislodge him. Her body wracked with fury and bitterness, all of which she held in for so long, now came out in torrents. His last words about not caring whether she lived or died weakened her. Tears slipped down her cheeks as she continued to try and free herself. Yet she knew she was not really putting any strength into her attack as she gave into feeling his hard, strong body pressed against hers.

Clarissa's rage did not affect Mel much. After all, he was used to displays of violence and hatred.

However, when tears ran down her cheeks, it completely unraveled any semblance of control he had. Making an inhuman sound, he grabbed her hand, pinned it to the ground then dipped his head down taking her lips in a brutal kiss. Mel's action was nothing more than a violent display of his inner turmoil, an attempt to punish her for what she was doing to him, the lack of mastery he had over his body when it came to her. His tongue thrust against her mouth, forced hers open and dueled with hers in an age long dance.

Clarissa was about to throw more insults at him for making her feel so much when all speech was halted as his lips pressed against hers, his tongue invaded her mouth brutally and yet, it was exquisite. Her body betrayed her, all anger, all heartache dissipated in that moment. Mel had thought to punish her with such a forceful display and yet it only made her body cry out for more. His other hand roamed over her body, gripping flesh as his mouth continued to assault the softness beneath him. His original thought process backfired on him, for as soon as he touched her lips, his body roared to life with such force that he shook from it as he drank from her lips with a hunger that bordered on insanity.

The gem's custodian moaned softly against him and wondered what she was doing. Her mission, duty, destiny all faded away into nothingness as he took up every emotional space she had with his body roughly pressed against hers. She could feel him hard against her hip and she knew this show of force was just that, a show.

Her body, stiff at first, softened, leaned into his and fueled the raging lust he already felt. As Mel ground his hardness into her hip, he deepened the kiss. His one hand massaged her scalp while the other moved to cup her breast, the tip already hard under his fingers. He growled deep in his throat at her eager response, berated himself for the stupidity of what he was doing yet unable to stop. Her scent enveloped him, invaded his senses and stirred his desires.

She tried to understand all that was happening and how her body seemed to respond better than her mind. She left her arm still plastered to the floor before her hand slid to his back. She could feel his corded muscles as they flexed against her, touched her body and set it aflame. Lust, desire ripped through every shred of her being. His hardness tantalized and teased her. She could feel her own juices pooling between her legs in response, her stomach clenched in anticipation and promise of what was to come. He took her breath away with his kiss, her body shivered to the sound of his growl, responded to him in ways she never dreamed possible. Her nipples taut, strained as her entire being gave in to the feelings he elicited from her, feelings she did not think she would ever have and for this one moment in time, she relinquished herself to this pleasure.

Her compliance urged him on. Mel kneaded her breast before he flicked his thumb over the hard tip, satisfied as she arched into his hand. Slowly he ground his hips against hers, let her feel his hardness, the intense force of his desire for her. He wanted to devour every inch of her soft, lush body until he was sure they were both sated and spent. Releasing her lips, his tongue trailed down her neck, dipped into the curve of her collarbone.

Azamel nipped and suckled on her flesh, tasted her soft skin. Resting on his elbow he moved his hand down the nape of her neck to her back, pressing between her shoulder blades as he lifted her chest to his waiting mouth. His lips closed over a hard nipple, sucking on her through the thin fabric of her shirt. The deep moans escaping his throat rippled over her flesh as his teeth scraped over her taut tip.

His breath became as erratic as hers and his head swam from the intense pleasure.

Clarissa could not help but squirm under him, rubbing herself against his hard body she almost swooned from pure ecstasy. Intense, erotic, blissful, none of these adequately described the feelings that radiated throughout her, burned her skin and boiled her blood. She hissed in air, gasped as he touched her body that was rapidly becoming extremely sensitive to his. She arched herself into his mouth, guided by his hand on her back. Shifting slightly, she let him peruse her body for all she could manage was to clutch onto him. Emotions swam through her and she delved into feeling only this moment, only him.

Closing her eyes to the intensity, her mind brought up the vision of his desire for the stone. The guardian's eyes snapped open as comprehension dawned on her. Despite how erotically wonderful this felt, his body against her, her body begging for his, she knew, *she knew* that he was using her to get the gem. Everything in that moment fell into place and she wanted to weep at the realization. But she would not give him the satisfaction.

She let her anger and her sexual frustration build and she used her wolf strength to push him back.

Once he was off of her she rolled to a standing position her arm outstretched, her palm up in a stay back gesture. "Nice move," she growled. "I know you want the stone but I am not that easy of prey." Clarissa caught her breath and slowly stood fully erect. "I admit I did not see that coming."

Azamel skidded across the floor as she jumped up and assumed a defensive position. Frowning at her, his mind gradually registered her words and actions. Rage, blinding in its intensity clouded his mind as he realized what she accused him of. Slowly he rose to tower over her, his demeanor suspiciously calm as he addressed her, his harsh breathing all that betrayed of his inner turmoil. "You think that was all an act, a way to get you to give up the stone?"

He had to use every bit of self-control to not snap her neck right there as disappointment overwhelmed him. Mel thought for the first time in as long as he could remember he would feel the pleasure of another, feel the warmth of someone that knew what he was and not have it matter to them but it was all a lie! His body shivered at the effort it took to keep from ending her life. "You are the blindest person I have ever met and given my age, Sweetheart, that speaks volumes. You want to get yourself killed? You don't want my help? You just got your wish." With a wave of his hand, Mel sent her back to her home in New Orleans.

Only when she was gone did he liberate the violent storm that raged inside of him. He needed to unleash the tempest that she had caused so easily. Mel flashed to his dungeon and the chamber of wicked creatures he had captured through the eons. He grabbed the whip from the demon torturing the sick fuck they threw in here a century before. Shock registered on the guard's face before he left in haste.

The look on the executioner's face promised dismemberment to any stupid enough to cross him at this moment. He let loose his fury at the demon hung from chains, his body released the rage he felt towards Clarissa on the creature sent here for his crimes against humanity. The beating and torment continued as the floor became stained in the creature's blood and Mel's sweat. After what seemed like forever Mel stopped, his limbs ached from the exertion, his lungs burned. With dead eyes Mel looked at the creature that had peeled the skin from his victims and laughed while he ate it in front of them, now limp from the punishment he received at the executioner's hand. Unable to dredge up sympathy for him as Mel remembered why he was originally brought here. He tossed the whip aside and left the room, instructing the guard to get rid of the mess made of the being inside.

Azamel flashed to his room and into a shower, trying to wash the scent of Clarissa away. Afterwards, he felt more in control of his emotions. The dead stoicism has returned and he wandered towards the grand hall deep in thought. So lost in his plans he subconsciously found himself in the room Clarissa had used. It drew him like a magnet, a strong pull to something of her, even if it was just the lingering essence of her presence. In pure frustration, Mel rubbed his hand over his face before he looked up to notice her backpack still on the floor. He growled deep within his throat as he looked up at the ceiling out of sheer frustration and cursed. "You are the cruelest fucking bitches every created."

He continued to rant at the Fates for their constant intervention as he picked the bag up and was immediately assaulted by her scent. Mel's body reacted instantaneously and that set him off on another round of expletives about body parts that appeared to have a mind of their own. Sighing finally at what he had to do, Mel first checked to be certain the dagger is still inside. *'Why would it not be? If it were not, it would only give her another reason to call me a user and liar, so best to be sure.'*

Making sure the backpack was secure and the dagger sheathed inside, Mel traced Clarissa's essence and frowned as he sensed her back in the jungle. Hating the bad feeling that washed over him, Mel teleported to the jungle to materialize by her side and in front of the ugliest mother fucking demon he had seen in a long

Chapter Four

Clarissa jumped back when Azamel who suddenly appeared beside her, ready to attack this new threat. When she realized it was him, she was stunned. She had felt betrayed by him when he sent her to her apartment in New Orleans, surprised he even knew where her home was located. She had collapsed to the floor and wept softly once she comprehended what he had done. She failed yet again.

Mel had the dagger, Xon had the other half of the gem of power and she was without anything and everything. Her heart shredded. Mel had called her blind. Granted, her visions were never one hundred percent, yet was she wrong to distrust his motives? She saw how he looked at the dagger, saw how his eyes gleamed at the stone.

She also remembered the way his kisses felt. They were brutal, hard then soft and devouring. Again her body betrayed her, for just the thought stirred her body to life and craved more of his touch. But he threw her out and without her gear. *'What the hell did I expect?'* She growled low to herself, adding even softer, *'I cannot care about him. He is using me. He was just manipulating me to get to the stone. Now he has half of it and I handed it to him on a silver platter.'*

She snarled, wiped her eyes as she stood, made her way to her closet and armed herself heavily. Once she changed into a camouflage outfit, she flashed back to the jungle, sword in hand. She would kill the demon named Xon and then somehow, some way she would get the dagger back from Azamel and make him pay for her weakness towards him. Make him pay for starting to care about him knowing he would do nothing but hurt her.

She had teleported back to the jungle in hopes of picking up Xon's trail, even if it was ethereal. Instead, what she came across was another demon that seemed to be on the same hunt as her and he was not at all thrilled to have competition in finding Xon and the gem of power. The creature immediately attacked her and she successfully defended against him. They were just preparing for a second round when Azamel appeared by her side, seemingly ready to fight the creature that stood before her. She could not have been more astounded than if she saw a pink hippo in a polka dotted bikini dancing the hand jive in front of her.

Azamel quickly assessed the situation and observed that Clarissa's arm was slashed and bleeding. He knew instantly this demon was not friendly. Mel's eyes bored into the creature, blood red as he moved to stand in front of Clarissa to shield her with his own body.

"I have looked into your soul. You have committed no crime worthy of judging, until now. Give up this foolish quest and remain free for another day. Attack and I will be forced to convict you for crimes against the magistrate. Sentence would be one hundred years of hard labor in the dungeons of Turano."

The demon stood still as he listened to the judge. He knew as long as he was not caught he had a chance to get the gem. He would therefore have the power to protect himself from any penalties but he had to get the stone and he could not obtain it if he refused to fight for the possibility of having it. The promised reward was too great to let the opportunity slip through his fingers. The creature materialized a fire ball and threw it at Azamel's chest sending him flying back into a set of trees lost among the thick brush. "I think I will find and claim the stone for myself regardless."

In the flash of an eye, the creature was in front of Clarissa towering over her. He slashed across her chest before she had a chance to blink or register he was there. She was down before she realized what had happened, bleeding profusely. She struggled, her breath became raspy as he slashed at her again. She was to slow to avoid him as a result of his first attack. She gasped, a tear running down the side of her face.

"Sorry Mama. I failed. Sorry. Forgive me."

The demon stood over her and laughed. Then he sent a bolt of electricity into her body, just to watch her change from wolf form to human and back again in utter agony.

Azamel transported before the creature. The demon gaped at him, shocked at Mel who appeared out of thin air. "Close your mouth, your breath is even worse than your body odor and trust me, that is pretty bad. You have been found guilty of attacking the magistrate as well as an innocent. Sentence is to commence immediately."

The creature snarled at Mel who relished the thought of attacking the demon and ending his miserable life but concern for Clarissa won the battle that raged inside Azamel's mind. He berated himself for giving a shit about her at all. Mel lifted both hands and before the demon could move he blasted him fifty feet away into a group of trees and shrubs. Mel waved his hand again and could hear the haunting screams of the demon as he was pulled into the dungeons of Turano to begin his sentence. Mel did not waste any time as he grabbed Clarissa and transported her back to his home.

Azamel laid her down gently on the bed in the suite he had provided for her as her body still battled to hold a steady form. He gripped her shoulder and sent a jolt of electrical current into her body causing the molecules to realign and settle her. She flashed to human form and thankfully kept it. Clarissa was still pale and shivered slightly. It was only then Mel noticed the wounds where she was hit. He held his hands over her body and healed the inflictions that caused her such agony. When at last her features relaxed and her breathing calmed, Mel flashed a bowl of water and a cloth to gently wipe her face.

Satisfied that she was comfortable and out of danger, Azamel placed the backpack next to the bedside table. When she awoke, she would see the bag and the dagger inside. He traced the back of his fingers over her soft cheek, a wistful expression on his face. With a last glance at her still form, he pulled a chair near the fireplace and sat down where he could keep an eye on her and the fire simultaneously.

Waking up with a roar of pain, Azamel looked around as he realized he was in the chair in front of the fire. He leaned back but as he did an agonizing pain ripped through his body. *'What the hell?'* Mel looked down and saw the blood dripping onto the chair fabric.

A huge gash peeked through a tear in his shirt, blood flowed freely. He had been so concerned about Clarissa being wounded in the jungle he had not noticed his own injury until now. He laid back and took a deep breath.

"Oh great, just fucking great! Damn, this day is just getting better!"

Mel's roar woke Clarissa. Her eyes fluttered open to stare at the buttressed ceiling of a room she recognized belonging in Azamel's home. The hearth blazed sending the only warmth within the otherwise opulent suite. But Mel was in the room and that mattered to her most. She scrambled to him, saw his shirt sliced and soaked red with his blood. Concern and worry creased her youthful features as she rushed to his side and knelt beside the chair. "Lay still, I can heal you."

Breathing through the pain, Mel kept his hand on the gash to try and staunch the bleeding. "I will be fine, it is nothing. Are you okay?" Mel looked at her concerned.

"I am fine. I seem to be constantly thanking you for saving me. Now, will you please lie still so I can see what I am working with here? Stop being a big baby and let me clean the wound and then heal it." Clarissa flashed in a bowl of water and a cloth as she pulled his shirt aside. She had to tear the material in order to get to the wound itself. Then taking the wet cloth, she gently wiped the blood away so she could see the extent of the injury.

Clarissa knew she could have just healed him straight away but for some reason, she *needed* to see how bad it was.

"Okay, sadly you will live."

The guardian looked up at him from her kneeling position as she teased him softly. Holding her hands out over his wound, she closed her eyes and let a soft, blue light emanate from her palms to spread over his wound, slowly mending and repairing the torn tissue and skin from the creature's fireball.

Azamel hissed at her none to gentle handling of

his injuries and let loose a string of expletives that would make a hardened criminal blush. When the wound was healed and the blood cleaned away, he laid back and breathed hard. His skin had an ashen hue to it and his whole body shivered. "I need to feed. The jungle took a lot from me."

"You should probably eat. Do you need my blood?"

Mel sent a mental message to Shara. *'I need to feed.'*

The judge shook his head at Clarissa. "Thank you for healing me, love, but nothing you have can sustain me food wise. I asked Shara to bring me something. Would you like to freshen up? Maybe a shower before dinner?"

Clarissa looked up to see Shara enter the room, her hands empty. Removing the water and cloth, she stood suddenly feeling a bit awkward. "Um. Yeah. That sounds like a good idea."

She spun on her heel as she nodded to Shara. Quickly she passed the servant woman as she made her way back to the bathroom to leave the two of them alone in the quarters she was assigned. Clarissa grabbed her backpack as she entered the lavish room, shut the door and leaned against it, sighing. *'Get your head in the game girl and to remind you the game is not the dating game.'* She shook her head, stripped and headed to the shower.

Mel frowned at Clarissa's hasty exit. He took the goblet from Shara after she materialized it and drained the contents in one gulp then held it out for more, his eyes bright yellow and his stomach cramped from need. When he finally felt sated, he gave the goblet back to Shara and dismissed her. Azamel sat up and stared into the fire, his mind kept drifting back to the jungle. *'Clarissa's powers are highly volatile and very closely tied to her emotions. She will need hard training to control them.'*

As Clarissa stepped out of the shower dripping wet, she let the air around her raise goose bumps on her skin. She grabbed a towel and wiped her face as her mind wandered to what they just went through and that he came for her. He felt her need him.

Why did he intrigue her so much? What was it about him that set her body aflame with just a look or a light caress? Was it because she could not ever have him? Talk about impossible situations? Talk about losing her focus on her destiny to dream about being with a man that, that what? Saw her as a child, a burden, a damsel in distress? She growled softly.

She could fight on her own. She taught herself and made it this far without him or anyone else. However then she remembered she was almost killed by that demon. She was not prepared. She was not as good as she thought. Or was she just distracted with anger for him! She needed his training, what he could teach her and yet the thought of spending more time with him worried her.

She sighed. *'Gods grant me help in making it through this ordeal and steel my heart against wanting something I could never, should never have.'*

Drying herself off, she quickly got dressed and curled up in the huge winged back chair to wait until she was sure Shara was gone from the room.

Azamel felt restored. Having sent Shara away, he got up and walked to her bathroom door. As he knocked on it, he called out to her, "Clarissa?"

She lifted her head. "Come in."

Slowly he opened the door and saw her sitting in the winged back chair. He walked over and sat in the one across from her. "You were magnificent in there." He looked away as if embarrassed to have confessed so much.

She blushed as she saw him look away, despite

the compliment. "Thank you. I just did what I had to, nothing more. I owe you my gratitude for coming in and helping me out. It's kind of nice to have my own body intact once again."

He nodded and gave her a long stare. "You have many powers but they are yet too unstable and too closely tied to your emotions. I can train you, if you want me to?"

He wondered why he kept asking but he wanted to help her. He wanted to know that she was safe and would survive for the additional trials she would have to cope with as time progressed. Others would come for the stone and therefore her.

Clarissa let her eyes lower under his gaze, felt her cheeks redden slightly. Working with him meant spending more time with him and there was a part of her that thrilled with the thought and another that cringed with it. She knew the more time she spent the harder it would be to be alone again when this was over. She rested her head against the wing of the chair, her legs already tucked under her form since before he came in. She looked lost in the big chair, small, uncertain. "If you please, I would appreciate your guidance."

"Dinner is served." He stood up and held out his

hand to her. "I am sure you are hungry? We can discuss your schooling over the meal."

She hesitated on putting her hand in his, yet the need to touch him, to feel his warm skin against hers was strong. He had shown courtesy to her, of which she appreciated. Gently she put her fingers in his, uncurled from the chair and stood. They were almost equal in height and still his presence seemed to dwarf hers. "I am hungry, thank you." Clarissa let him lead her to the dining hall.

Mel smiled and threaded his fingers through hers as he led her to the feasting room. Once there, he pulled out her chair and motioned for the staff to begin serving them. After the drinks were poured, the judge saluted the wolf, "To safely getting out of that hellhole jungle and to finding Xon quickly."

Clarissa smiled sweetly and held her glass out to clink with his. "May we succeed when we do meet up with Xon." She sniffed, putting her nose lightly in the air.

"It smells divine." She picked up her fork and started to eat. "So what do you have in mind for guiding me? Have you prepared others before?"

Mel started eating and nodded. "More than I

can remember, love. I am very, very old as I think you have ascertained." He chuckled. "I have a training room here that would give us the space and equipment we shall utilize. You are welcome to stay here while we practice."

"Other than maybe gathering a few personal items, no one will miss me." She immediately wondered if she should have told him that but shrugged off her apprehensions. "Thank you for the offer of your hospitality."

He raised a brow at the former comment but made the choice to ignore it after feeling her palatable discomfort. "I will take you to get what you need or you can just ask Shara. She will provide you with everything you require."

"I would prefer my own items please." She took a bite of her meal, chewing thoughtfully. "This is very good." Clarissa looked up at him as she paused in her eating. "Has Shara been with you long?"

"Seems like forever. Yes. We can get your things after dinner and whatever else you might require."

"That will be acceptable. I will even buy you dessert for your trouble." Clarissa frowned slightly, picking her food with her fork. "I wonder where that demon, Xon is with my stone."

Mel took her one hand in his. "Eat, get your belongings then we will work on your abilities. He is not going anywhere."

Her haunted eyes looked up at him, his hand still closed around hers. "What damage has he done?"

He released her hand and let her finish her food. "I don't know, I would suggest you try to track him but we saw what happened the last time we tried that. We need to stabilize your powers first. I have my demon chasers out there and if he moves out of line, I will know about it. When you are ready, we can go get your things."

Clarissa nodded and pushed her plate away, suddenly losing her appetite. "I am ready as soon as you are. Thank you." She dabbed her mouth daintily with her napkin, set it on the side and sipped her drink while she waited for him to finish.

Azamel set his glass down and stood. He moved quickly to pull her chair out for her and held his hand for her to take so she could rise. "Let us be on our way then."

Again, she was mildly surprised at his gentlemanly manners. Lightly, she placed her fingers into his hand and stood. He flashed them back to her apartment in New Orleans. She released her hand from his as she moved to the closet to grab a bag for the items she planned on taking with her. Her focus was to gather some personal effects, some additional weapons, her sword and a couple of exercise outfits. Once completed, she turned back to him.

"I am ready." Then she stopped and thought for a moment. "Oh Wait." Clarissa quickly jotted a note to her employers so they would not worry overtly. She grabbed the only picture she had of her family from the dresser adding it to the items already in her bag. "I am ready now."

Azamel silently watched her gather her belongings and the thoughtfulness of leaving a note. *'Family. I had that once.'* He shook his head to clear the melancholic thought, nodded and took her hand. He transported them to her quarters within his home. "Once you are ready, meet me in the training room. Down the hall, five doors down to your left" Mel then dematerialized from her presence.

Chapter Five

She took some time to put a few of her items away. She took the picture and placed it on the nightstand by the bed. She sat on the bed and stared at it for a few minutes, lost in thought. She wished her family was still around and this was all just a nightmare she would wake up from. But alas, it was not a dream. Changing into exercise gear, she followed Mel's instructions to the workout room and knocked as she pushed the door open. "Azamel?"

Dressed only in black pants, Mel practiced with a long wooden staff. Going through the moves, he twirled the staff around, stepping and breathing through the warm up exercises. He did not hear her enter until she spoke. As he looked up and gaped at her outfit, he missed a move and hit himself with the staff on the side of his head.

He felt his face heat at the mistake. Frowning as he rubbed his head, he motioned for her to enter.

As she stepped in, she bit her lower lip to keep from laughing at his misstep when he saw her and softly cleared her throat. Her eyes roamed his bare torso. His six-pack ripped abdominals and flexing arm muscles she saw while she watched him move enticed her to taste every bit of skin and then some rather than practice.

"Should I have brought a weapon?" her voice was unsure, hesitant. She had never worked out with someone who was not her family and certainly never one who was as distractingly delectable as this hunk standing before her.

Recovering quickly, he tossed her another wooden staff. "I have seen you fight, I know you have skills. This part of your schooling is about controlling your emotions. Anger is your biggest enemy and it seems to affect your ability to focus your powers." Mel slammed his staff against hers. "Now attack me. Or are you afraid, little girl?"

Clarissa knew the little girl remark was an attempt to get her riled and it would not work. She remained calm, her breathing controlled as her eyes narrowed in preparation for an attack. She swung her staff, knowing he was expecting her to give a full frontal attack. She had other plans however. At the same time she swung, she dropped her knees and swept his feet out from under him, before she spun to put the end of the staff halted at his throat. "Good enough, old man?"

Mel slammed the staff away with his and rolled over, hitting her legs which sent her to the floor. He flipped up and twirled the staff. "Not by far, sweetheart! That was such a girly move! If that was a demon, you would be dead." He stepped back and leaned on the staff, "Is that all you've got?"

"I doubt it. I would have taken its head off before he realized he was on the ground." With one wrist, she spun the staff like a whirly gig. Stopping it, she embedded it onto the floor, using the leverage to kick him back, hitting him square in the chest. Dropping back to her feet and before he had a chance to recover, she scissor kicked him. By the time she landed on her feet, he had rebounded and met her attacking staff. The wood clunked as they collided and she looked into his eyes, panting slightly. "Taunting me really won't work much."

He parried the stick against hers and held it down while he moved to be nose to nose with her. "Is that not what you should have done when your home was attacked? Maybe if you took a few heads off instead of running like a fucking coward they would be alive today." Mel shoved her back and twirled the staff. "Maybe we should end this now. Cowardice disgusts me."

Her breath caught in her throat as his words hit her harder then she believed possible. Pain shot through her heart and she wanted to crumple, before fury took over and all she saw was red, hatred mingled with heartache. She swung the staff out with the speed and agility of her species, quickly. She hit his knees then his side. Her attack kept coming strong, sure but it was not enough. Even though she pushed him back, it was not enough.

She no longer saw him standing before her. She saw only a target for her anguish and despair at everything she lost, at all she would never have and it blinded her. She saw him approach her again, lifting the staff to meet hers and she swung her arm out and used her telekinesis. She pinned him to the wall, three inches off the floor. An invisible force enclosed his neck and squeezed. She swung the staff like a bat and hit him over and over again.

"I am not a coward!" with each sentence came a swing that contacted with his body. "I tried to help. I didn't know how! *I am not a coward!*" Finally she collapsed into a heap on the floor, releasing him and let him drop.

Mel gasped for breath as she relinquished the pressure from his neck. He forgot how strong she was as she battered his body giving him a full reminder. Her face contorted as rage bled from every pore. When her fury was spent and she fell on her knees, he breathed hard and swallowed past the soreness in his throat. He moved slowly to where she was on the ground and nudged her over with his foot. Calling on all his reserves to keep his face impassive even though he ached for her sorrow, he looked upon her with no sympathy in his hardened gaze. "That is what will get you killed. Now get up."

Clarissa snarled at his coldness to her pain. She stood and kneed him in the groin. "You would be dead now, Bastard."

He grabbed his crotch as she kneed him hard.

"Fuck!"

She pushed his bent over pained body away from her then kicked him hard in the gut to watch him bounce off the wall. "I have killed many and I am still here!" She swished her arm to the side and threw him to the other side of the room, crashing again into the wall.

"You wanted me pissed?" She shimmied her

breasts. "Well come and get it you damn asshole." Again, she flung her arm out using her telekinesis and threw him to the other side of the room. "I am just getting warmed up, you imbecilic asinine, pathetic excuse of a man!"

She went on a rampage and literally tore into his body as her emotions completely took over. He decided he had enough of this and shielded himself from any more of her blows. An invisible wall came up between them and blocked any further attack. It gave him a few seconds to recover before he threw a hand out that blasted her flat on her back and pinned her down. He walked over slowly as the ache in his groin was still very prominent and looked down on her captured, squirming form.

"Stop! Listen!" He held a hand over her. Slowly his fist closed increasing the pressure on her to remain still. "You hit me because I allowed it. Never delude yourself that there are not beings out there that could not kill you with but a thought. Fighting helps you to focus, keep your body honed and keeps away most of your attackers. That is *all* it does. Your skills lie in the powers that are unique to you. They are what will give you the edge over almost every other being. That will be your survival. Your biggest weakness is your inability to control your rage and

concentrate on your powers. You can hide your
agony, your shame, your fury as much as you want
to. There are some of us out there that can see it no
matter how well you keep it hidden. Some of those
do not have your best interest at heart and they will
use that against you. They can only use it if they see
how it affects you and how it lets you lose sight of
your gifts." He sighed, let the pressure drop and held
out a hand. "I did not want to do that and I have no
malicious intent, yet it was very easy for me to rile
you. Can you imagine if it was someone else and they
fought back?"

She knocked his hand away. "Do not touch me
you *horrific beast!*"

Clarissa rolled away from him, got up and
backed away, her body ached painfully from his
throw but she refused to give in to him one iota.
"You want to prove I am a fly to you, end it now. You
want to use my pain against me, here is your chance.
If there is something out there that can kill me with a
thought what the hell good is it if I learn to fight
better? And my *best* interest at heart? You are so full
of it! You are a stagnant douche bag of green slimy
testicle warts! You *allowed* me to hit you? Gee, how
fucking generous of you! My powers are unique to
me? Well, let me alert the newspapers on that

revelation. Now here is one for you. My powers are mostly passive, *Moron!* I would have thought you would have realized that by now!"

He dropped his hand and refused to be angry at her. "Very colorful, Clarissa, the purpose of this was to get you to manage your emotions enough to release and control those abilities. Once you achieved that, you would not have to fight beings such as I, you would have the tools to avoid them or annihilate them." He gave her a small nod. "I thought you were ready, I was mistaken." Mel walked out the room without so much as a backwards glance.

Furious, Clarissa tilted her head back and screamed in fury. Her telekinesis powers built, causing the weapons to embed into the walls of the room as room shook and shimmied. It made it feel as if an earthquake struck the training facility and reverberated throughout the abode. After several minutes, her power surge faded and she slid to her knees, her face in her hands, exhausted, weak, thoroughly worn out. She felt too feeble to stand much less do anything else.

Mel kept walking down the hall towards the hearth in the main room. He ignored the sounds of destruction that came from the chamber she was in. He knew she needed to vent her anger, hurt and to approach her now would only make matters worse. It was times like these that the judge detested what he was and what he did.

The guardian was an innocent and one of those whom he was honor bound to protect. Her pain was necessary for her growth but it was not pleasant to hear nor was it something he relished putting her through. He sat down in front of the fire, stretched his achingly sore muscles and waited for the tempest to calm.

It seemed like an eternity that she stayed within the destroyed area but she knew from her were-wolf powers it was only thirty minutes. She was extremely abashed. She acted like a two year old throwing a temper tantrum. Slowly, on shaky knees, she climbed to her feet and tried to stop her head from spinning. Grabbing at the wall, she paused to steady herself. She slowly made her way to that hideously cold, eerie room with the fireplace to find Azamel there.

Not wanting him to know how weak she felt, she hesitated, straightened her outfit, lifted her head high and strode into the room despite her legs desire to fold under her. She figured she was pale but there was nothing she could do about that and thanks to the dancing lights of the fire, maybe it would not be so noticeable. "I guess I own you an apology. I should have not acted so immature."

Azamel looked up at her. He could not help notice her condition and the pride with which she held herself. He turned back to the blaze within the hearth, quiet for a few moments. "I want you to get the stone back and learn your powers." He added very softly, "And not hurt inside anymore."

Clarissa frowned as Mel looked away from her and spoke so quietly. She lowered her head in shame. "I would like all of that too. I know you should not even be bothered with me considering the way I behaved." She took a softly sighing breath. She backed up slowly as she made her way back towards the room he assigned her.

Mel materialized directly in front of her to prevent her from walking away. "I was a total dick and I am sorry. Your true enemies will not be as considerate and they *will* kill you." He could tell she doubted him and he reached forward to grab her shoulders. "*Look at me! You can do this! You are stronger than you think!* You survived more than many could endure and you are still loyal to your calling. Don't ever think pain does not cripple us all at one time or other."

Clarissa gazed up into his blue eyes. "I know

every creature suffers heartache of one sort or another. I do my best but as you have shown me it is not enough. I do not know how to put it aside or use it either. I do not understand."

He kept his hands on her shoulders. "Close your eyes and breathe slowly in and out. Concentrate on regulating your breath. All you hear is the sound of your heartbeat. Now open your eyes while still only hearing your own body. Nothing else matters, no sound, no object, nothing. You have to be quiet inside. When you can achieve that calmness and peace in the midst of any battle, you will succeed."

"This is kind of like I do for Tai Chi and Ninjutsu. Center myself and call for a calm. *This* I can do." She closed her eyes and meditated, listening to her heartbeat as she breathed in and out slowly.

"Good, now see your home. It is burning, they are screaming for you to help, the death blows fall and the blood runs in the streets. They call you! Clarissa, help us! Why? Why are you running? No, don't leave us." He saw her waver and her eyes flickered. Mel gripped her shoulder harder and spoke calmly. "Focus!"

A tear slid down her cheek from her closed lids. She tried to breath, to clear her mind, yet she saw her brother Johann, telling her to take his new red Ducati and escape. He wanted her to save herself, while he distracted their attackers. Big brother to the end, he would do everything possible to see her survive. She softly whispered his name, "Johann."

Briefly Mel closed his eyes against the anguish she felt as it washed through him with their connection. He wished he could take all this away but if she did not deal with it and learn, she would be killed. He lifted one hand and wiped the tear from her cheek. "I know it is hard to do this. Breathe and see it play out as if you were watching a movie. You are not emotionally involved. You are an outsider gazing at the scene."

His hand against her cheek gave Clarissa clarity somehow, his words gave her direction. Giving a subtle nod, she tried to focus again and worked to leave her heart out of it. She started over again, from the beginning.

Chapter Six

She neared her home as she came in from the fields. The screams and cries easily heard as she approached the building. She paused, not sure if she heard right or for that matter what might be happening. After a moment she turned the bend and saw her little corner of the world being torn asunder by a rival pack of were-wolves. She was astounded. Never in a zillion centuries would she have thought anything like this would have happened, or was happening.

Her first thought was her family, her nieces and nephews, still infants, still pups. She was already close to the house and entered without being seen, without being noticed. The carnage dropped her to her knees and made her violently ill. Trying to recover, she heard a commotion out back and it sounded like her brother Johann. Scrambling to her feet, she dashed out the back door, only to see him and another of her brothers, Ian being attacked by more wolves. She cringed as Ian went down under the onslaught. Johann's gaze fell on her. He sent a mental message for her to take his bike and run. So their attackers would not see her, Johann ran in the other direction, allowing them to give chase. *This was not real.* She kept telling herself. *This was a nightmare.*

Johann swung at the wolves attacking him, trying desperately to keep them occupied so Clarissa could escape. She backed up slowly, wanting to escape this horror. She needed to run, get the bike and get out of there as she was told to do. She knew that Johann would sacrifice himself to make sure she survived and she would not disgrace him by letting herself get caught and therefore killed. She would not let him die in vain because she failed to live.

However, it was too late. One of the wolves smelled her fear on the wind and turned in her direction. Snarling, his fangs dripped with saliva and blood, he charged at her. Clarissa ran, skidded and bolted as fast as her feet would carry her towards her families shed. Located inside was the red Ducati that Johann had recently brought home only a week before. He had taken her for a ride shortly after he purchased it. Johann showed her how to drive his new machine, held her while she tried to maintain balance and encouraged her to keep trying.

As she ran to the motorcycle, she felt the heavy paws of a wolf pouncing on her back, pushing her face to quickly meet the floor of the shed. The wolf's fangs sank into her shoulder. She felt the sinewy muscles and tissue being torn. Clarissa screamed and kicked, tears overflowing her already dampened cheeks. Her hands reached out as she tried to find anything to dislodge the furry beast off of her. She found a crowbar. Her fingers stretched and tried to roll it towards her for a better grip.

It was just out of reach and kept rolling back slightly, until *finally*, she was able to grasp it. Getting a good grip on the tool, she twisted at her waist and whacked the wolf in the head with as much strength as she could muster. She repeated hitting him until the intruder's fangs on her shoulder loosened and slackened.

Squirming out from under him, she quickly scrambled to her feet. Her one side slightly limp from the shoulder bite, blood dripped down her arm. As the wolf staggered toward her she growled as she kicked it hard in the jaw.

Her father had made sure his children knew how to defend themselves and encouraged them to take martial arts. She always thought hunting with him was more fun than practicing kicks and hits but she was never more thankful now that he had insisted she learn.

Once the wolf was back far enough, he took a running leap at her again. This time she caught the beast in the chest with the pointy end of the crowbar. Utilizing the handle of the bar, she flipped the wolf to lie alongside her. The furry beast became unmoving except for a few twitches as he expelled his last breath. She sank to her knees. Clarissa took the life of a living creature. She should be sorry, remorseful and even regretful but she wasn't. He helped to kill everything she loved, everyone that was her life. They were gone. *All* of them gone.

She ran to the bike, rolled it out and revved it up. Jumping on the seat, she sped as fast as possible to escape. A few more wolves tried to chase her but could not keep up with the motorcycle. She skirted around those who tried to halt her progress. She kept running and never looked back. She knew she could not afford to. She was blinded mostly by the tears which streamed down her face but she did not stop. She prayed they would not find her, while she also hoped they would so that they would kill her and she would once again be with her family. Her life was destroyed in a matter of minutes.

In the hall, his hands still on her shoulders, Mel could see the pain and sorrow on her face as she played out scenes she never wanted to think about again. Her body already weak and power drained, his grip pretty much held her up. Slowly, she opened her eyes. They were green and dark with untold agony. "It hurts to remember. I had not fully allowed myself to do so until now." Her lower lip quivered. "I miss them so much." Clarissa's face contorted, she wanted to cry though she tried desperately not to. However, she was too weak, too exhausted to prevent the tears from building, her emerald orbs becoming pools of glistening iridescent green.

Azamel contemplated whether to push her or let her rest for a while. The emotional pressure of what they are doing would take its toll on anyone. Since she had always buried her emotions, this was even more difficult. Forcing someone to deal with something like this was not anything Mel was comfortable with but it had to be done. Her very life depended on it, her sanity. Gazing into her windows to the soul made the decision for him and he pulled her into his arms.

That small action seemed to break a dam inside her and her tears flowed freely, wetting his shirt. Her body shook as sobs tore through her. He kept his arms around her, gently rubbed her back and just letting her get everything out of her system. When at last she started to quiet down, he just held her until she pulled away and looked up at him with teary eyes.

"What happened to your family is a terrible tragedy, one that someone your age should not have been exposed to. It is not your fault. The fact that you survived and they did not is also not your culpability." He lifted her chin with his finger. "I am very sorry I had to do that in there and my deepest condolences for your loss. I do not like what we have to do in order to get that stone back but you as the guardian will have all kinds of creatures coming at you over the years. The sooner you prepare the better." He gathered her back in his arms and just embraced her tightly.

"I thought I was pretty prepared to begin with. Though I admit I was distracted a bit when I came upon that demon in the jungle. However it was not my family I was thinking of. I was angry with you." She held him loosely, comforted by his arms wrapped about her. "I have held the tragedy of my family in for so long. I never realized, until now just how much I avoided."

"Sometimes in order for us to heal, we have to break down all the barriers we have erected over the years. Walls we built to protect that deepest, darkest part of our soul, the part that we can agonize over repeatedly. We are so afraid to hurt again that we would rather hide the pain, bury the feelings that paralyzed us when something happened that we could not comprehend. We built a chamber and placed all the hurt, anger, resentment and hatred in there and locked the door."

Mel continued to rub her back in a soothing motion. "The problem with doing that is, we hold on to that despondency. Those aches are never gone nor dealt with. They are just lurking underneath for an inopportune time to resurface. They slumber until the day comes that we have to face them, the day that an event forces us to open that chamber. Those emotions were dormant yet growing in intensity because we unwittingly fed them by allowing them to linger. The day they escape, they hit us with the force of a freight train and if you are not prepared or strong enough they will maul you on the spot or at the very best, force you to your knees."

"Like now? Everything, every molecule of my being aches in missing them, in what happened to them, in not being helpful or useful in saving them." She moved closer to him, let his arms wrap about her and wept softly on his shoulder. The pain of her loss tore through her. Feelings of being alone and hermitical overwhelmed her.

"I am trying my best. I just don't know how. I was unprepared for this duty. I was untrained for these obligations. All of this was unknown to me until just a few months ago. What am I supposed to do to protect it? For centuries it was safe and hidden. I get the duty and twice it has come into danger of being taken by another. I am useless. I have failed my responsibilities twice!"

Clarissa clung to him, the temper tantrum a half hour ago on top of this forced emotional release of remembering her recent past tore her mentality to shreds. She doubted she had much strength left to fight a fly at the moment. Hell, she could barely stand without his support, though she would not let him know that.

Though she wondered if that was even possible, for he seemed to know everything she thought and felt. Trying to calm her nerves and settle down her emotions, for she was sure this austere man did not want to put up with youthful, womanly tears, she took a few deep breaths and backed up slightly, wiping her cheeks with the palms of her hands, "So now what?"

Mel released her and stepped back, realizing she needed the space. He walked over to the hearth and placed one hand on the mantel to stare into the flames for what felt like an eternity. "We will have to continue doing that until you learn to control your emotions. I know this will be hard for you but it is your one Achilles heel, a fragility your enemy will exploit."

He walked back to her and materialized a black orb in his hand. The ball shimmered as if a dull light pulsed from within its core. "I think this may aide your growth. You look into the orb and remember that day. The memories will be captured within the ball and anytime you want to review it, tell it what you wish to see and it will replay it. This will help to analyze what you see without feeling it over and over again. You need to look at it and find something in your memories that will ground your feelings, a *happy* inspiration or an emotion that will help you control those that cause you to lose concentration."

Mel relinquished the ball and closed his hand over hers as it held the sphere. "This will be one of the toughest things you will ever face. I am not going to lie to you. It will also be that which you need to confront in order to succeed and to be the guardian I know you can be." Mel released her hand and with a slight incline of his head faded out of the hall.

Chapter Seven

She held the orb and watched him fade from the area. She really hated when he did that. She looked into the black inkiness of the sphere and moved back into the room to sit down on the couch in front the burning hearth. Looking at the winged gargoyle skeletons on either side of the mantle she shivered slightly, grateful she never met the moving skinned beasts that those frames belonged to.

Taking a deep breath she looked into the darkness of the circle she held in the palm of her hand. Once again she recounted that day in her mind. Every nuance, every emotion, every word that she could remember, from the cold crispness of the day and watching her breath escape in wispy smoke from her mouth and nose. The ache and terror she felt when she saw everyone she knew dead, dying or fighting a hopeless battle against wolves that seemed determine to obliterate such a peaceful home outside a small hamlet.

She remembered everything and when she was done, she put the orb down gently despite the desire to smash it into a million pieces within the burning hearth.

At this moment in time, she detested Azamel for making her do this, for forcing her to relive that moment over and over again. Getting up, she paced the room, her mind a whirl with everything since the moment she escaped the horrors of that day. She had survived! She had made her way in a world she knew nothing about. She learned how to fight and how to persevere. No one ever used her memories against her. No one distracted her like Mel did, or made her as angry. No one had hurt her as badly since the day she lost her family.

Why did she continue to let him do this to her? What power did he wield over her that she was so susceptible to his very presence? How had he managed to worm his way into her heart that she was affected so easily? Curling up on the couch in as small of a ball as she could make herself, she looked at the fire, finding it more pleasant than the globe that held her tormented past.

*****

The creature's face dropped like a bloodhounds, sagged deeply, slack with pain. If he was not bound, he would likely topple over, cracking his skull on the floor. A nerve in his shoulder twitched uncontrollably. The muscles in his leg clenched. Blood dripped down his body, some fresh, some sticky and drying. His body marred by cuts and bruises, some so deep the bones are exposed.

His moans and screams reverberated through the caverns, the torturous cries of one begging for a merciful death. Azamel walked over and grabbed him by the hair. The blood drenched strands stained his fingers as Mel pulled at it. He bent down and snarled in his face.

"Where is he?"

The creature's whining response was barely audible through his cries for mercy. He coughed up blood and some unspeakable matter.

"I don't *know!*"

The amount of torture the creature endured and still denied any knowledge of Xon convinced Mel of his ignorance. He deserved mercy after the days of agony, despite the lack of it the creature showed to his own victims as he tortured them in pleasure.

With cold, unfeeling eyes, Azamel allowed his fingers to elongate into a sharp, deadly claw and ripped across the condemned's neck, almost severing his head.

As his body sagged, Mel cut the bounds and the body dropped in a bloodied mess to the sanguine stained floor. He watched until the last guttural sounds died and the body became limp and cold. He deserved more than he got for the pains he inflicted on others. Mel just wished he could have gotten the information they needed as well.

With a slight shrug, Mel left the room and the desecration behind. He could have flashed directly to his private space but he needed the exercise to ground himself. He felt nothing for the life he ended. A creature such as he deserved to die for his heinous crimes.

However, the frustration and anger because he failed to trace the fucker that had the stone caused him to be on edge.

Clarissa stood and took the black shimmering ball with her, deciding to return to her assigned quarters. As she stepped into the hall, she saw Azamel walking. His clothes were splattered with blood and other viscous fluids. She felt sickened at the thought of what he did to get that way. Averting her eyes, she headed back towards her designated suite, wondering if that was what he ate or what he played with. Either way, she did not want to know.

As Mel glanced up, he saw Clarissa retreat hurriedly to her room. He cursed inwardly, realizing his appearance must have shocked her. Deciding not to approach her in his current condition, Azamel stalked to his chambers, flashed naked and got under the hot spray of the shower. The water cascaded down his body and he relished getting the stench of decayed demon off of him. After a long time under the warm jet, he got out, dressed in black slacks and an Oxford shirt. His hair still damp from the shower but feeling much better overall, he headed to her room and softly knocked on the door.

Clarissa's mind continued repeating how she saw him in the hallway. She tried to block it out. Hell she had seen worse, so what was the big deal now? It could be because she thought of him with a certain mystique and did not know what to make of his recent appearance? Perhaps she just so shaken up by the fact that he appeared so disheveled in his own home that took her by surprise? Changing out of her exercise outfit into a halter and mini skirt, she sat on the couch in the room as she eyed the orb when she heard a knock on the door.

"Come in."

Using his powers to unseal the door which swung open in one silent move, Mel stood there as still as a statue as he just stared her. Deciding she would not bolt in terror from his earlier appearance, he slowly moved into the room and approached her.

"Have you been using the recording globe?"

She frowned and bit her tongue to prevent eliciting a snide comment. Instead she put on a stoic demeanor and looked at him all shiny and clean. "Yes." As she stood and advanced on him, she lifted her chin. "Does the teacher want to check my homework?" *'Okay, I could not resist being snide after all.'*

He gave her a peeved look. "This is no joking matter. I am giving you all the tools to help you in this quest and you mock me?" He curled his lip and snarled at her. "You are entirely welcome to leave and do this on your own sweetheart"

"Joke, you think I find having my heart torn asunder over and over a *joke*?" she snapped back at him, spinning on her heel to stalk back to the couch. "You are one odd creature Azamel, if you think I find this entertaining in the least. Furthermore, I am sick and tired of you calling me sweetheart and love and anything other than my name. Those terms are something that is said to someone you care about and it's quite obvious you tolerate me at best."

She gazed upon the orb. True it held her memories of her family's death but it held more too. That of what Mel's very presence wrought in her. This was the reason why that demon got the better of her to begin with in the woods.

Azamel infuriated her in a way she never felt with anyone else. He soothed her as easily with a light touch. She did not even want to think about his kisses or his scent. She didn't want to think about how good his hard body pressed against her, those steel arms wrapped about her waist as he pinned her against him excited her like none had before. She growled low. *'Gods help me if he ever discovered the truth of my feelings for him.'*

He tilted his head to the side, bewildered at her reaction. Mel probed her mind gently to find the source of her sudden anger. He was surprised, elated and also irate at what he discovered. A complication, a twist he did not expect, a ramification she did not want. Though he understood her desire to remain alone as a result of her responsibilities, Mel found that he was extremely disappointed she would not make room for him in her life. Considering that he also could not have a companion, it shocked him to discover how upset her feeling that way actually made him.

"That orb can both help and destroy you. I gave it to you to help you heal from the tragedies of your past and protect you from being weakened by those memories when you are forced to face them. If you fail, that stone will be lost or worse found by our little friend and then my dear Clarissa, we are all fucked. I am much more than an odd creature." He rubbed his palm over his face and muttered against his hand. "More than you want to know but I am committed to saving you and that stone. We cannot choose our destinies nor can we always run from it. We can learn to face it or we die. We live in a world where the term dog eats dog gets a whole new meaning. Friends are few, enemies are aplenty and alliances are what we need for survival. Trust no one, rely on no one and kill before getting killed. I have lived longer than your mind can calculate and believe me, the sooner you adapt to those rules the easier it will be to fulfill your duties *and* survive."

Mel moved over to the bookshelf, peering at the volumes with his hands clutched behind his back. He added in a soft whisper. "The object holds memories unique to the one handling it, it is yours to deal with, yours to analyze, yours to relive. Anyone other than you looking into it will either see their own memories or just a black mist."

"Well, you may think of me as a petulant child compared to you but have you ever had to do this. Experience over and over again something that shattered your whole self. I was better off using it as strength, a power to reckon with."

She plopped on the chair, crossed her legs, her arms folded over her chest and took a deep breath, trying to calm herself in his presence. Maybe she should just go, put distance between them and yet, she knew she needed the help. There was no way on god's green earth she was going to be able to get anywhere near Xon. The demon she ran into in the jungle was not as strong as Xon with part of the stone and that demon would have killed her. He would have torn her to shreds had Azamel not appeared when he did. Why did he? Why was he there to save her when he had kicked her out because of her accusations? What was his game? She knew he wanted the gem for himself, though keeping it out of the demons hands was also important to him. She knew what the stone did, how it called to others with the promise of ultimate power and ultimate destruction for those who opposed them. He may say he is helping her and part of that was most likely true yet, she sensed the deceit in him as well. So she spoke up.

"Survival is a funny word. One can exist but not actually live. I prevailed in that attack by the jungle demon that I should not have because I was focused on something else. Why were you there? Why did you save me at the most opportune moment when you already had the knife? You could have easily found Xon and got the other half of the gem of power with me out of the way. Why?"

Mel snorted at her words but kept his back to her as he spoke, "Pray you never discover what I have had to endure to exist, the pain and torture I have seen and inflicted in order to maintain some semblance of sanity. So yes, I know all about perseverance." He turned around slowly, his eyes burned into hers. "I have proven to you on more than one occasion that my intentions in helping you are noble. We can discontinue this alliance if you continue to second guess my every move. The fact that I did have the opportunity to get the stone and chose to help you should be proof enough of my commitment to assisting you. I do not however take lightly to my methods or my reasons questioned and you would do well to remember that." He held out his hand, palm up when he noticed she was about to interrupt. "You have a choice. Give me the orb and I will take you home. You are on your own to deal with the situation as you see fit or two, we continue on this path together and we may have a positive outcome for all."

She found he was very good at avoiding the actual questions posed. She stared a moment at his hand then up into his eyes, seeing their pale blue coldness with no hint of warmth or concern. Why did she expect any? Why would he have any attachment to her? At best he might be interested in a sexual alliance, he was certainly enthralled with the stone and despite it all, she hated herself for just wishing there was something more solid, more stable with him. That she could have something tangible with someone. Yet, she knew, especially from his many comments, he was not interested in being with her for anything more than training. He could not invest anything to her emotionally, just as she could not. She closed her eyes as that reality hit her head on.

Weakened emotionally already, she could not bear the reality of this thought as well. "So what is next, oh great masterful one?" Clarissa meant for her words to come out sarcastically but instead they were soft, weak and almost forlorn.

"Next, you need to can the sarcasm and get relaxed. You should appreciate the break in order to handle our work out later." He paused as he walked past her to access the door. "Make sure you rest well. You will need it. I want to see if the spheres powers have helped."

She sneered back at him, waited until he walked past her and whispered under her breath, "Bite me." She knew immediately she should not have said anything at all but damn it, he infuriated her like no other. He would not bend one iota and she would be damned if she let him know how he was affecting her.

Her words snapped the tight cord he had over control of his inner demon. The pent up frustration he had to deal with around her, the emotions he dared not explore, the feelings of concern he should not have for this woman forced the demon inside to claw at Mel. It wanted out, wanted to hurt her for causing this turmoil inside him. The demon was not used to be denied and Azamel was at a point where he did not or could not contain him any longer.

Mel grabbed her neck in a vice like grip,

squeezing slowly. His eyes turned the luminescent yellow that mirrors the twin dragons on his throne. The heat from the change burned his eyes and he felt the tingling sensation as his skin darkened blood red. The voice that left his lips was not the one Clarissa had heard from him since she had met him in the woods days before. Instead, it was a deep, demonic sound that echoed through the otherwise silent chamber.

"Do. Not. Push. Me. You have no idea what I am capable of, little were."

A slight tremble rushed through the room, shook the walls and rattled the chandelier. A grey haze clouded his vision and he had to fight the urge to snap her neck as the demon desperately screamed at him to do. Mel tossed her across the room to land in a heap on the mattress before he whirled around and exited the room, a harsh wind followed in his wake that slammed the door shut.

The wolf starred at his retreating back until the door closed with such force it knocked the picture frames off the wall. She gasped for breath, rubbing her neck as she stayed in the crumpled pile she landed in, shifting only slightly to draw into herself more. She hated him. She hated this existence she found herself living day to day and wished he had ended it as he was so wanted to do but just a moment ago. She had never seen anything like him and for once, he actually scared her. Not that he would kill her but of his true demon essence, his true visage, the sound of his voice echoed around the room in his fury.

She had pushed him hard before but never as much to have caused this kind of a reaction. If nothing else, she realized she was nothing to him. She had not touched any part of him and for some stupid, foolish, unknown reason, this was what hurt worst of all. So she had to harden herself, again. Push out what she foolishly let in, *him*. Learn what she needed. Get the stone. Get on with what little life she had. Only right now, she did not move from the heaped ball she was in on the mattress

Chapter Eight

Azamel flashed to his secret room as soon as he left her. The snarling beast within needed to be free and Mel always retreated to this private place where the demon could lash out without Mel hurting anyone he might truly miss. As soon as he entered the chamber, Mel dropped his guard and allowed his true visage to form. He hated this part of himself. He detested that his parentage took over. The demon always punished Mel for being forced into submission. Mel lay on the floor and let the guttural growling demon take his anger out on him.

The creature transformed Mel's body, ripped through his flesh in a way that would inflict the most pain as it was torn apart. While the demon clawed his way out, blood splattered, marring the walls and mixing with older stains. The pain was excruciating and Mel's screams echoed throughout the realm, the agonized sounds piercing in their intensity. The cries were eventually drowned by the deep, demonic laughter of the creature as he finally tore himself from the body that served as his host. Azamel's essence remained but as long as the beast was loose Mel could feel but was powerless to do anything other than wait out the storm.

Lost in her own self-pity, Clarissa did not realize she was hearing anything but her own heartbeat. Then slowly, the sounds of agony and pain, of untold screams of horror pieced through her revelry. She was going to ignore it. After all, how Azamel got his jollies was his concern not hers and he made it perfectly clear she was to stay out of his business. What he ate, what he was, anything and everything about him she was not to know. *'Then again, the tone, the pitch, was that? No. It could not be, could it? Was that Mel was screaming in such distress?'*

Climbing off the bed, she headed out the door of her room and tried to follow the sound. She soon realized that she needed her alternate form if she was ever going to track down his whereabouts for the sound reverberated too much for her to find him otherwise. She called upon her shifters powers, let her white fur sprout from her skin, her nose elongated, her ears and teeth grew and became pointed.

She bent over to all fours and swished the tail she now had. The wolf bent down and used her nose to follow his scent. His occasionally loud cries guided her when his odor became too confusing to follow. The smell of blood was almost overwhelming and she had to concentrate on his unique scent to continue. It led her down corridors that were dark and dank, passage ways that seemed to be honed out of the earth itself. The sounds became more prominent, the torment more piercing as she approached a sealed door. The emanations came from inside but she saw no way in. She transformed back to her human visage. She called to him through the wall, wondered if he would even hear her or could answer.

"Azamel? Azamel! Tell me how to get in. Let me help you!" The answer she received was more shrieking. She took her hands and searched the entrance, looked for a way to open it, pounded her fists against the roughhewn rock.

Having not been inside she could not flash in, or she might flash into someone or something. She heard the demon voice that had threatened her life, wanted to tear her to shreds. She realized that the demon Mel warned her was inside of him had gotten out. Mel was paying the price. She knelt by the room and softly talked to Azamel doubtful he would even hear her.

"Mel. Let me help. Let me in. Allow me help you fight this demon of yours. Azamel, tell me what I can do. Please Mel, let me help."

*****

Days passed and Clarissa spent every moment at that spot outside the room Azamel was holed up in. She did not eat, barely slept. *Yeah, cause she could really sleep with that horrific sound of agony constantly piercing her eardrums.*

She chatted to Mel, talked to the beast, though in most cases, she felt as if she were just soliloquizing. Clarissa ignored the demon that conversed back to her, threatening to eat her entrails in disgustingly poignant details that churned her stomach, hence the not eating. It knew she was there, wanted her and wanted out. Still she stayed as close to Mel's side as she could. Even though he might not want her there, to know this part of him existed, to see or in this case, hear him, she refused to leave him alone.

She could not help but she refused to go, regardless of how long this lasted. She knew, beyond a shadow of a doubt that he had suffered like this many times in the past. For once, he was not going to go through this alone. She would be here and when he finally emerged, she would help him or he could tell her to go screw herself. Either way, she was not going to leave him until he appeared from the room.

For days, the beast clamored and tried to break free from the chamber it was imprisoned in. When his anger was finally sated he reluctantly retreated. Azamel was able to obtain control again and healed his shredded body enough to *consider* leaving the chamber. Yet, it still took two additional days for Mel's body to knit itself together into some semblance of a human form. Bruises and horrific scars dissected his skin. It would heal eventually as it always did. Azamel was weak more so than he had been in an extremely long time.

The demon was slumbering once more, his fury spent. The room was eerily still, like a tomb that had been forgotten over the years. The air musty and thick, condensation clung to any inanimate objects it found. The yearning was a constant and palpable ache deep within Mel's being. It was a need unfulfilled, which was maddening since for ages all his desires had been achieved with a mere thought. All except the need to be free of this beast and what would happen if he ever became too weak to control him. For centuries that was all Mel desired and focused on, controlling the beast and finding the sustenance he needed to achieve that control. However, after practically an eternity of near omnipotence, Azamel finally felt something else missing in his existence.

It was once long, long ago that he did have needs and wants, though these lessened with the passage of time. His family's lineage was the guardians of these creatures whose original, primitive, physical forms were despised more than any others. A creature so vile, none would speak of them or their true nature. The creature Mel was required to host as a result, was Azamel's curse which he had to bear. Mel's passions and lasciviousness were quelled over the centuries of control and he became immune to the suffering as well as the cares of others by closing his heart to anything other than his job. However as he laid on the floor trying to mend himself enough to actually leave the chamber, he could not help but think, once, just once in his entire existence someone would be waiting for him. That someone had blond hair and eyes so fantastically green that they sparkled with an inner light.

Mel threw the last thought aside with revulsion. The memory of his origin was a source of repulsion that he would have expelled long ago if it were not for the fact that the demon would never let him forget that he was there, lurking in the shadows, waiting for the chance to break free. Mel was not usually given to emotion but he felt a wave of annoyance, curiosity and then even nostalgia. He mulled over what could possibly be amiss in his place through eternity. Surely he could find some inner peace? Surely he deserved someone to care for him after all the centuries of his servitude? The judge shook his head to dispel the image and got up. His broken body protested at the effort to move. With weakened knees, he made his way out of the enclosure only to almost fall over the still form outside the door.

Moving with the swiftness of her werewolf linage, Clarissa caught him as he almost fell over her. "Mel!"

She wrapped an arm about him gently and teleported him to the quarters he had assigned her.

Gently, she laid him onto the bed. Holding her hands out, she closed her eyes and let a soft blue light emit from them, ameliorating him. He was too strong, too powerful and far too wounded to heal him completely. She was much too young to harness the intensity it would take to wholly meliorate him but she could help ease the worse of his condition. The wolf desired desperately to inquire as to what happened, what occurred behind those doors, why he looked as bad as he did but she knew he would not tell her and probably only get upset that she asked, so she remained quiet. Once she rehabilitated him as much as she could, she obtained a bowl of warm water and a towel to gently wash him.

"Are you hungry? I can call Shara or whatever her name is to get you what you need to eat."

Images flickered through Mel's mind as memories of the past and the present ran through his head. He tried to examine his emotions, realize that it was the driving force for most of his actions of late. When he got angry, he warred against those who infuriated him. Love, affection and nurturing were nuances he did not understand. Her gentle care of his wounds both confused and scared him. How could a creature such as he ever expect any affection such as that which she now bestowed on him?

Mel's everyday life was filled with conflict. Disputes were settled with violence. Adversity was omnipresent in his world. He saw creatures who embraced the joys of life when times were good. Although ardor drove much of this positive behavior, there was something else that lay at its foundation. It was the need to give, an act of unselfish charity. Some called it love.

Azamel had omnipotence and infinite knowledge but he could not share his life with anybody. He could not help or guide anyone when it came to love. What was missing in his life went beyond mere loneliness. He was used to being lonely, used to walking solitarily. He sometimes had the need to give of himself but there was no one to give to. He turned his head to hers, his eyes barely opened. He was weak like he had not been in centuries.

"Call Shara, I need sustenance." He turned his head back and closed his eyes to rest while he waited.

She heard his request and immediately called for Shara. As soon as the woman appeared, Clarissa told her to bring Mel's nutritional requirement for him. Once the servant retreated to procure the necessary comestibles, Clarissa gently propped up Mel with pillows so he would be able to take what he needed without hindrance and then continued to wash him gently.

"I am sorry I cannot heal you more but when I regain some of my powers again, I will give you another healing boost. Shara is on her way with your food."

She wiped the cool towel across his brow but paused as Shara came back. Knowing this was something else he considered private, performed without her hanging around, she put the towel and water aside. "I will be right outside while you eat." Nodding towards the other woman, Clarissa slipped out the door and leaned against the wall, her arms folded. Her mind was awhirl with thoughts and emotions.

She was doing it again. She felt compassion for him, concern. Why did he continue to worm his way into her soul when she should care nothing for him and all his secrets? Still, he was a creature who suffered and she never would turn her back on that. This time it was more than that. He had done a lot for her and she cared about him. Hell, if she were truthful, she knew she was in love with him. Banging her head against the wall, she frowned as she realized she was a glutton for punishment and heartache.

Mel followed Clarissa with his eyes as she left the room, puzzled as to why she retired so easily. He was so weak that she could have exploited any desire to remain and retrieve the answers he knew she was curious to secure. He allowed Shara to raise the goblet to his lips and let the sustenance he so desperately needed flow into his mouth. With each drop that slipped past his throat, he felt some of his strength return but only after the third helping did he feel a semblance of the humanity he desperately wished to have. With a curt nod, he dismissed the servant.

Shara silently moved to the door but paused just before she was about to exit. "Is she worth it? Is she worth what you are doing to yourself?"

Mel spoke slowly, enunciated every word, his tone deadly, "You forget your place, Shara."

Shara knew that inflection, the soft dangerous voice that normally preceded dismemberment and death. "Forgive me, my Lord. I am merely concerned for your well-being." Keeping her head down, she exited the room.

Sighing wearily, Mel closed his eyes as he felt the nourishment flow through his body. He hated weakness in any form, especially in front of his servants. But he also realized she had a valid point. Shara had been with him for eons. Her servitude was impeccable. Never had she questioned his orders or what he did until now. Why did Clarissa open his heart? How did she touch a part of him that had been extinct so long he was sure it was dead, buried and turned to dust? His heart ached for her. A muscle he thought only pumped his cold blood through his veins. He found himself wondering what it would be like to have her by his side throughout the otherwise lonely, monotonous days. Was she worth it? He wished to the seven hells he knew.

Clarissa saw Shara as the woman left the room and gave her an odd look as she passed by the wolf. The guardian shrugged it off. She understood Shara might not appreciate her being here and in truth could not care what the female thought. She did not care much for nosy help who ransacked her

personal items earlier either, so the feeling of
distrust and disdain were mutual. Clarissa's concern
was not Shara but the man that was lying inside.
Slipping in, she shut the door behind her and headed
back to one side of the bed. Seeing his eyes were
closed, she proceeded quietly to let him rest. Moving
a chair near the bed, she curled up into it and rested
her head on the protruding corner of the wing-
backed chair. She started to take his hand in hers and
caught herself. *'What the devil got into me?'* She
folded her arms and shut her eyes, reposed as well.
Once rejuvenated, she would be able to mend him a
bit more. Opening her eyes again, she made sure he
was comfortably tucked in and then settled herself
back down by his side. At least this time there was no
stone wall between them and no snarling demon
threatening to rip her to shreds and play with her
innards before he ate them.

Chapter Nine

After a long, fitful night, Mel opened his eyes to a cold room. The fire in the hearth had died and the chill was evident. He willed the fire to start again and within minutes the room was warm and comfortable once more. As he turned his head, he spotted her curled up in a chair fast asleep. The executioner laid there for a very long time just watching her. Shame, guilt, remorse and many other unmentionable emotions ran through him.

She aided him even after what she beheld, who she observed he could become. It was humbling yet frightening. No one other than Shara had ever seen the monster and he knew the fear in her gaze every time he got irate. Mel manifested a blanket and covered her. The movement caused her eyelids to flutter open. Time suspended as they both just stared at each other. Azamel finally managed to speak despite his parched throat, "How did you find me?"

She heard the dry crackle of his voice and generated a glass of water as she moved over to him.

"At first I followed the screams. When I could no long distinguish from which way they came, I shifted to wolf and used my nose to follow your scent." She tapped the side of her facial protrusion. "Wolves have really, really good sniffers. I feel stronger again today. I can help you heal a bit more."

'Fuck! I never thought that room would ever be found.' He laid back and closed his eyes for a moment, his mind whirling with what she must have seen and heard. He shook his head slowly. "I just need to rest more. I need to get to my chambers." Mel tried to rise from the mattress.

"Let me try and improve your health a bit more. Let me help." She blocked his way and gently pushed him back to the bed. "Sheesh, you make a worse patient than a doctor." She held her hands out over his bruised and torn body once again, able to improve the majority of bruises and ease the bulk of his pain before she had to pull away. Turning her back to him, she knew he wanted to escape her presence, so she started to busy herself with folding the blanket up that he had covered her with and brought the chair back to its original location.

Feeling much restored, he slowly got up and moved to stand behind her. His hand hovered over her shoulder, almost touching but not quite. After a long pause, he dropped his hand and turned towards the exit. He had never felt this vulnerable or exposed to anyone in his entire existence and he was lost as how to proceed. "I- I'm sorry," his words were barely audible as he moved to the door.

Her head popped up and she looked at his retreating posterior. "Sorry, for what?" Clarissa stepped closer to him, unsure how near to get. Not because she was scared of him but because she was uncertain how far she could push him. Skeptical of what he felt towards her if anything. She was hesitant of everything that consisted of him. He did not scare her. She may not have seen his true visage but she heard it for days on end. She took another hesitant step towards him. "Sorry cause I got a taste of what you really are inside? Okay, I cannot truly say I have seen worse but, so what? I still stood or laid or sat by your side and guess what? I did not care other than you were suffering and I could not help. Or are you sorry because I cannot fully heal you all at once, even though I am using what power I have to do what I can?" She shrugged. "I am sorry I am so young and cannot heal you completely at one sitting. I do what I can and hope it's enough. Sorry that I have seen you weak for a change? Well guess what? It's nice to see you are vulnerable and not just an aggressive cocky omnipotent being. So do not be sorry. You have nothing to be sorry for."

She watched his back, his shoulders almost appeared to slump slightly at her words and she wondered if she bruised his already macho ego further but she was at a loss here and could only speak her heart. Even knowing it might not be enough. She stared and realized she was afraid, not of him but of her feelings towards him, of how vulnerable it made her feel and most of all of him walking out that door as if she mattered nothing to him what-so-ever. That somehow she had not touched his heart in some small way like he touched hers.

Mel turned on her as fast as his bruised body could manage and grabbed her shoulders, slightly shaking her. *"Enough!"* He added in a softer, almost defeated tone. "Enough."

The demon took more out of him than he could deal with and he was not sure if the events of the past few days, the responsibility of keeping this woman safe or the reluctant softness she stirred within him caused him to act in this insane manner. He pulled her hard against his chest and growled near her lips. "I never meant to hurt you." With a defeated sigh, he slammed his lips on hers. His hands moved into her hair, moved her head to fit his seeking mouth. He kissed her with an uninhibited need, breathless gasps escaped him and his tongue begged for entrance so it could duel with hers. Her hands instead of pushing him away moved over his shoulders to fist in his hair, pulling his head closer to her. Liquid fire coursed through his veins as he tightened his hold on her.

His head filled with the scent of her, her very essence permeated his senses and he could no longer resist the allure she presented. He had to have this woman, no matter the cost. Tonight, Mel was too weak to resist her. His body shaking, he pulled back from her lips. His Adams's apple moved as he swallowed hard and looked deep into her eyes. He spoke in a soft, almost pleading way, terrified she would say yes and more afraid if she said no. "I want you."

His shaking anger touched her heart and she hated herself for letting it get that far but then he softened and touched her and her whole being soared. His kisses were like melted butter, slipping warmly throughout her body and she could not help but bring him closer to her. She heard his words and her body responded immediately to his request. She stepped back from him. She could almost see the hurt and disappointment in his eyes, virtually crippling him until she pulled her shirt off and slipped out of her skirt, leaving only the skimpiest red lace underwear imaginable on. Moving up to him again, she tore his shirt open, sending buttons flying in all directions. Then pulled him back towards the bed, wordlessly giving herself to him, needing him desperately.

Mindless with need, Mel allowed her to pull him toward the mattress, her eyes warm and inviting. When she paused at the edge of the frame, he shrugged out of his torn shirt and let it drop soundlessly to the floor. His hands trembled slightly as he moved them up to cup her lace covered breasts. His eyes followed the trail of his hands but gazed back at her face when a gasp escaped her lips as his hands folded over her soft mounds. He maintained his gaze as his thumbs caressed her nipples in slow circles, bringing them to rock hard peaks.

He moved his hands around her back to release the clasp of her bra, letting her breasts spring free from their lacy confinement. His fingers immediately moved back to cup her again, the peaks scraped against his palms.

With an agonized growl, Mel captured her lips again, desperate, seeking. His need scared him but his whole being was focused on possessing this woman. Mel's tongue delved into the deepest recesses of her warm mouth while his fingers fondled her. He pulled his mouth apart from hers so he could push her back gently to land on the mattress behind her. Her breasts jutted, her hair fanned over the bed and she stole his breath away. He pushed his knees between hers, opening her up to his hot gaze. After a slow desirous look over her beautiful body, he covered her with his form and kissed her almost brutally. He moaned deep in his chest as he kissed her hard and deep, his hips ground against hers to let her feel the full extent of his arousal.

Her hands daintily glided over his skin. A part of her mind worried he was still too sore, hurt too much but it was a fleeting thought as his lips claimed her again, his hands touched her body. She slipped her own down his back and along his waistline to the front of his black pants. Undoing them, she pushed them over his butt, her hands skimming over his ass cheeks and down the back of his thighs as she released him.

Clarissa thought about when they were near this point once before and she had not trusted him the first time, pushed him away. It seemed so long ago, another life time almost, yet so much changed since then. He had proven himself over and over and she knew, whether right or wrong, she wanted him. Her body ached for him, needed him and this time she would not deny either of them. Her hands continued to rub his back and slide up to fist in his hair holding his mouth against hers. She explored every crevice, tasted his warmth, breathed in his intoxicating scent.

Her body quivered under his touch, her nipples stiff and aching sent chills throughout her body. She even felt the deepest recesses of her womb tingle with anticipation. She felt the juices of her desire pool between her legs caught by the merest whisper of red lace, the only barrier left between them. Lifting her knee onto the bed, she opened herself up to him, giving his body a chance to cover and press against her, skin to warm skin. She could not get enough of him, did not want to have this moment end. She nipped at his lower lip. She lifted her hips and let the lace rub against his hardness. She moved her bent leg over his hips to draw him in closer and moaned softly as his hands roamed her body, sending flames of heat to every spot he touched.

His lips tore themselves from hers and moved over her cheek on their way to nibble her lobe. His breath tickled the inside of her ear as he licked and sucked on her succulent flesh. His knee pressed against her core, the dampness from the scrap of lace covering wet his flesh. He impelled harder against her heat as his mouth moved down her neck, nipped her skin as he went. He pulled her arms over her head. The position lifted her breasts high, her back slightly arched. Mel's hands slid down her arms to cup her breasts and lifted them towards his waiting mouth as his tongue flicked over her tips, wet them, made them even harder.

Moving to her left, his teeth scraped over the engorged nipple before taking the pebble fully into his mouth. He sucked upon her breast slow and hard at first, his tongue swirled around. Her body writhed against him, skin against skin, flesh against flesh. Small shivers ran up his spine causing him to suck on her hard, dragging the nipple almost painfully into his mouth. His groans vibrated against her flesh, his eyes shut as his relished the taste of her. As he pulled back he watched her flesh bounce as he released her. He licked his way over to her other mound to pay it the same attention. The fingers of one hand move down over her stomach, pausing to swirl around her navel and then travel further to push into the waistband of the now damp lace covering her core. His middle finger pressed strongly along her swollen nub, ground against it in a slow circular motion. Her soft moans set fire to his blood. His cock expanded and throbbed in its intensity. His breath came in small pants as he feasted on her tender skin. As Mel's finger continued his toying with her clit, his tongue followed the path his phalanges took earlier. When he reached her lacy shield, he ripped the scrap off in one smooth motion and replaced the fabric with his open mouth over her secret treasure.

She arched and squirmed under him. As she opened her legs wider to give him full access to her body, she lifted her hips to meet his mouth. "Oh Gods, that feels so amazing," Clarissa gasped out, breathless from his attention to her body. Her whole being felt like it had lava flowing through her veins, he made her that hot, that needy. Her hands slipped along his back as he moved further down her body, to rest lightly on his head as he tongued her heated womanhood. Her juices flowed freely and she realized how much she had wanted this, desired him. Her whole body was alive with sensations that were almost foreign to her, sparking fireworks through her nerves. She writhed beneath him, pinned by the torment of the wickedest tongue she ever encountered. He moved his hands to lift her ass up, which gave him better access to her throbbing heat. His tongue moved in long strokes up and down her folds, rolling her lips around his tongue. He lapped at her sweet juices before he nibbled her nub with his teeth, scraping her sweet flesh with his whiskers. Her body could not resist the torture he gave her. He brought her need to a rising climax, a desperate release and gave his tongue what it elicited from the deepest recesses of her body.

Azamel drank every drop from her. He was so hard, the tip leaked a droplet or two of lubricant and he was not sure how long he could keep denying his own need. Her body called to him like a siren, irresistible. He raised himself up as her thrashing body almost undid his iron restraint. He moved up her body with a speed almost inhuman, grabbed her hair forcing her to look at him. His tip hovered at her entrance as he kissed her harshly, allowed her taste herself on his tongue. Mel lifted his head, while pressing very slightly into her. "Are you sure?"

Her eyes roamed his face as he peered into her eyes. His normally pale ice blue orbs were dark with a passion and lust she knew hers reflected. She had to pause for the question to register. His movements were so fast, so quick in shifting positions. It took a moment to realize he had moved much less asked a question. *'Am I sure? Gods what a time to ask!'*

Any walls she tried to put in place to prevent this from happening were torn down the instant his lips were on hers. There was no way she wanted out, or wanted to stop. Her body ached with desperate desire for him, dreamed to feel him inside, to be a part of her. It was like she was awakened, her body, her nervous system, her core, tingled, throbbed and craved his touch, his tongue, his arms about her, his manhood in her. She desired to surround him, be a part of him, just this once. There was a deep recessed part of her that knew she would become addicted to him if it came down to it but she did not care. For once, she would give into these primal urges that called to her very depth of being. She wrapped her legs around him, stared him in the eye and spoke distinctly so there would be no question, no second guessing, no doubt. "I could not be more positive of anything. I want you."

He closed his eyes and swallowed at the sudden lump in his throat. This was a turning point for both of them. It was not just a sexual act but a merging of two bodies and souls. Although he wanted this, it also terrified him to open himself up in such a way. His past liaisons were just a means to an end. But Clarissa was different. She touched him in a way he did not believe possible or could exist for a creature such as himself.

He held his breath for a moment before he thrust deep into her warm body. Her walls immediately gripped his cock as he immersed himself in her depths. The sensation threatened to overwhelm his senses and he kept still for a minute, to let the feelings wash over him and to permit her time to adjust to his girth. The small gasp that escaped her lips ignited his lust and he lifted his hips to pull slightly out of her before he slammed back in. His thickness deep within her heated core pulsated as he continued to penetrate deep within her hot sheath. Her legs wrapped around him, her heels dug into his clenching cheeks as he moved. He pushed his tongue into her mouth to mimic the deep thrusts of his body. One hand moved to grab her ass, squeezing as he rolled his hips with each entry. Faster and deeper as he felt her clench around his shaft.

She sucked on his tongue, a game of trying to catch it as he plunged into her mouth with the same intensity as his cock pushed into her core. Her hands gripped his shoulders and biceps as he rode her hard. Her need to release ever close but she refused to give in to such pleasurable heights again so easily, at least not just yet. She wanted to cum when she felt his hot seed rush through her channels and towards her womb. She wanted that to push her over the edge, push her beyond any control she might have. It was so difficult to hold on. His hand moved between them to touch and stroke her nub in time with all his other moves. Perspiration formed all over their skin as the pleasure built to a fever pitch, threatening to consume them both.

Her breathing more ragged, her body beaded with sweat, left rivets between her breasts. She touched his balls, already slick with her juices, massaging them as he pounded against her, "Oh Hell!" She tore her mouth from him, tilted her head back and gave in to the power of his cock that drove so forcefully into her while his hand massaged her nub to beyond any intensity of ecstasy. She could not hold on any longer. Unable to wait she arched her whole body rigid for a moment, suspended slightly above the mattress before she cried out. Shuddering in his arms, her juices poured from her, dampened her hand between them even more.

Her release hit Mel like a freight train and snapped his control. Time for slow will come later. His body refused to be denied any longer. He pounded into her with a fury bordering on madness, sought that ultimate release. Oblivion awaited and his body hurt for it. His balls tightened a moment before his cock exploded with a fierce shock and his hot release jetted deep into her body. The spasms and aftershocks rippled over his skin as his head fell back and a roar escaped his lips. When at last his body was spent, he dropped his forehead to hers just breathing. Mel's eyes were closed as he inhaled their scents mixed from the lovemaking. He captured her lips in a soft, slow kiss as he slightly suckled on her tongue.

Trying to get air in her lungs almost burned but she did not care. It was so worth this time with him. Who would have thought that she would end up here, naked, sweaty, under him, kissing him, feeling the rush of her ecstasy mingled with him in that edge of glory that lasted seconds and an eternity rolled in one. She was not regretful she gave herself to this, to him. Funny thing was, deep down she knew that this was where she was supposed to be. It might never happen again but this moment in time had to occur and she regretted none of it. She arched her body to his, tilted her head to lick at his lips and teased his tongue with her own in languid movements. She inhaled his scent deeply, tried to commit it to memory. He was still buried inside her, reluctant to leave the snug sheath, both of them twitching and pulsating in the aftermath of their blinding release.

Mel's mouth nibbled a trail from her lips down to her neck, licked her succulent flesh. His hand moved slowly over her shoulder, down her arm, over her hip to follow the curve of her thigh. He nuzzled the hollow of her throat before he traveled up to her lips again. His eyes met hers, still hot from lingering passion. He gave her a small smile. "Hi."

His lips blazed a trail across her satiny skin beaded with a light sheen of perspiration as a result of their intense activity. Her nails lightly traced patterns on his back. His eyes still slightly darker than she was used to, filled with a subsiding lust that she knew was reflected in her own green orbs, she could not help chuckling. After all they have been through, all they have done culminating in this sexual experience and he said hi? "Hi."

He could not stop gazing at her. His eyes trailed over her face as he took in every inch of her. Emotions warred inside him, awkwardness, tenderness and fear. His body reacted to hers in a way that was carnal, needy. Even after their play, he was not sated. Somehow he thought if he had her once he would get the desire for her out of his system. He realized, once would never be enough as his cock stirred inside her. He dropped his head and leisurely traced her lips before he dipped his tongue inside, slowly exploring her mouth. He moved his hips against hers, his body eager once more. Clarissa's mouth molded to his, matching his excitement. He felt his cock expand, growing inside her as his body quickly recharged.

This night was far from over and if they were allowed only one night Mel was damn sure he was going to make it memorable. Before she could move, he pulled out of her, flipped her onto her stomach and pushed deep inside her again. His one hand grabbed her hair to tug her head back towards his waiting lips. "I hope you are not tired, because I plan to feast on you for a very, very long time." He slammed his mouth back on hers with a fierce growl and thrust deep simultaneously, moved her body hard into the mattress.

She pushed past the concern that this man who actually started meaning something to her would be out of her life when the stone was recovered and the thought of losing someone else who had become important to her stole her breath away. She wanted this, him, so badly it permeated her senses beyond recognition. It was a hunger, a craving, an insatiable desire to have him, to feel him pounding into her ready and waiting body.

She moaned against him as he moved within her heated core with such ferocity as to make a wolf proud. His chest pressed against her back, his hand fisted around her long silken hair. She was impressed he was managing so well considering she had not thought she had healed him much from whatever ordeal he had gone through with his demon and yet his stamina, his prowess, his ability to take her so expertly proved her wrong.

She reached behind her with one hand to touch the back of his thigh as he moved within her. The other was used to maintain some semblance of balance. She pushed back into him, needing to feel him continuously, his balls slapping against her backside. Her breasts bounced freely with the pounding thrusts of his body against hers, the scent of him and their sex mingled in the air aroused her senses even more, lifting her up into the heavens. "Feast away. I can handle whatever you can dish out."

Her response fueled his appetite to such a point where he ignored the screams of his aching body, the agony in his muscles from the past few days of hell. Her walls gripped hard around him and sent goose pimples over his skin. His arms pushed under her to lift her frontal portion from the bed. Grabbing a pillow, Mel pushed it under her to lift her ass in the air. With him on his knees, he grabbed her waist as the new angle allowed him to go even deeper into her. His hands curled into her hips and slammed her back into him as he thrust forward and down. Her ass hit his thighs as he pounded into her, the heat and moisture pooled on his legs.

He played with her, shifted her from one position to another as if she weighed nothing. She did not mind. She was lost to the proclivity of his being inside. Her core was as hot as a furnace, gripping and throbbing around his thick, hard driving member that rocked her body across the cool pillow and sheets crumpled under her. Her nipples pressed against the mattress, rubbing with the movements that added to her torturous pleasure. The sheets still held his scent from his lying there and she breathed it in. Her juices and his seed mingled and slipped down her thighs from their last orgasm, sticky and warm. She thrust her hips up towards him, her head low and her shoulders back. She let him have his way with her and enjoyed every moment of it.

Her body's reaction was like a drug that invaded his body and caused a delicious delirium in his mind. She was about to discover demon lovemaking at its best and he hoped she could keep up.

He touched her and she soared in flaming heat. He thrust into her and she melted like butter, he pinched her hard aching nipples and canals of lava flowed faster through her veins. She was lost. She thought once she gave into him, her heat, her lust would be sated but she was so wrong. He played her body so expertly that she did not want it to end and wondered how long a semi-weak demon could keep this pace up. She prayed he would manage for a while yet, because she really could keep going.

He added a digit to her engorged nub. His hand covered in her sweet juices. Her ass slammed against his thighs as he rammed into her body, their breathing becoming labored. Deeper and faster, Mel sought oblivion within her channel.

She shut her eyes to just feel the gratification he was wringing from her warm, sweaty figure, his hands and fingers elicited simultaneous feelings throughout various areas of her form. Leaning back against him, she let herself go, cried out, clenching her muscles. Her body throbbed around his, her hand pressed against his rubbing her core, her head on his shoulder as she leaned back against him as she shuddered through her orgasm.

He felt her body tightened around his shaft as he threw his head back and roared his own release, the sound echoed around the chamber. He kept pumping until she wrung every last drop from his convulsing cock. When at last his body stopped quaking, he fell on the mattress, pulling her with him as his arms folded around her. Their breathing labored, he spooned her back and placed soft kisses on her shoulder. "You were incredible"

She curled up with her back to his front, his arm about her waist, trying to force air into her lungs. She smiled and looked back over her shoulder at him. "Not too bad yourself. How are you feeling? Are you okay?" She could not help but add to her words, despite her genuine concern for his well-being. He had pushed himself pretty hard especially after the ordeal of the last couple of days. "I didn't wear you out or hurt you too badly I hope."

Mel's body screamed at him as his adrenaline tempered with the completion of their activities. He should have waited before taking her but he could not deny what he wanted any longer. "I'll live." Snuggling against her, he tried to keep his breathing steady so as to not betray the pain that wracked his body. "I just need to recuperate for a little while."

Clarissa tilted her head slightly. "You're hurting. I can hear it." She shifted towards him as part of her felt awful for doing what they did. It was not because she wanted him as badly as he seemed to want her but because she knew he was unwell to begin with. Maybe she should have kept her mouth shut and let him walk out that door for him to recuperate but she never was one to keep her thoughts to herself and most times found words past her lips before she was even aware of it.

Maybe it was her fault for constantly pushing him but she did not want him to feel guilty for having seen who he really was, having beheld the demon inside of him, or having seen a part of him she truly doubted many, if any at all, had confronted. She was tired of the way he made her feel small and inferior sometimes. She was tired of the conflicting emotions from him. One minute he seemed to care, the next he was as cold as ice. But then, she was no better.

One moment she detested him and the next she wanted this, his arms wrapped around her, holding her tight. "Can I get you anything? Try and give you some more of my healing energy?"

He cringed inwardly as he realized she could sense his pain. He replied sleepily, "I just need to sleep, with you in my arms. Can we do that?"

She settled back against him. "Yes, we can do that."

Chapter Ten

Waking up slowly, Azamel took a moment to adjust to his surroundings. The fire still crackled in the hearth, creating pleasant warmth to dispel the chill that was always present in this realm. Clarissa was still fast asleep next him, her limbs entwined in the sheets.

He turned on his back to stare at the intricately carved ceiling. Mel's thoughts whirled as the events of the past week rushed through his mind. Last night was a mistake. He realized he could not afford to attach himself to anyone, let alone a young wolf emotionally scarred almost more than he was. With a deep sigh, he ran a hand over his face. They both had an enormous responsibility that they carried on their shoulders. The stone was too valuable to fall into the hands of the Xon or any demon. The world was fucked up enough as it is without having some demon with an inferiority complex taking over and fucking it up even more.

There were things that humans could never know about, should not know about as it would alter their very existence. She was the key to defeat Xon and Mel vowed to protect her. The feelings she stirred deep inside of him were a complication that he should not explore, could not analyze. Azamel's very existence was a threat to her and her kind. The beings Mel controlled and policed threatened every one of her kin along with everyone else who roamed the earth. He knew if his enemies found out about his care for her, she would be hunted to extinction and he could not allow that to happen. With a weary sigh, he got up, left a single pink rose and a note on the pillow. It read: *"Rest well, love, I have a few things to take care of. I will meet you in the training room at noon. M."*

Mel stared at her sleeping form for but a moment longer before flashing to his own chambers to clean up. His muscles were still stiff as a result of the demon clawing him from the inside, the scars faded but still visible on his flesh. Last night's antics also left him a bit tender as he had not been fully healed to begin with.

Feeling much improved, he dressed and materialized in the human realm. His informants should have some information by now. Xon could not hide forever. He would need to feed and the lure of the other half of the stone would force him to make a move soon. Mel would be waiting.

*****

Clarissa was surprised to have slept at all, much less so late. She slowly opened her eyes to find the bed empty save for a rose and a note. Languidly reaching over, she rubbed her eyes to read it. Her internal clock told her she had a half hour before meeting him. Sighing, she rolled onto her back and stared at the ceiling a few moments more. Last night was a huge mistake. She knew it. She thought if she did it with him she would have it out of her system. *Him* out of her system. However, all that occurred was she became more addicted to him.

Staring at the ceiling, remembering, she almost felt him still touching her, his skin against hers, felt him fill her and throb inside of her. Her body responded to those thoughts, those memories alone, already heating up again. Growling at herself and her body's betrayal, she crawled out of bed and took a mildly cold shower to wake up as well as cool her form down. Stepping out of the shower, she dressed in a pair of yoga pants that fell at her hips and a halter mid-rift stretch top that hugged her curves and left her stomach bare. Pulling her hair back in a ponytail, she headed to the training room. He was not there yet, so she began stretching to loosen up her muscles as she waited, her mind wondering what Xon was doing in her absence.

Mel watched her as she sauntered into the exercise arena his shade form not visible as he leaned against the wall. The piece of scrap she wore would mess with any man's senses. She moved like a dancer, controlled and fluid. His body became hard just watching her and he had to breathe slowly, focused to get his reactions under control. She turned to face the opposite wall from him and he materialized, clearly visible in the mirrors in front of her. Her eyes widened slightly as she saw him but she stayed silent

Mel walked up behind her until their bodies almost touched, his eyes keeping hers captive in the mirror.

"Don't stop."

As she began to execute her exercises, he coordinated his movements with hers. They stretched and twisted in perfect harmony, his eyes never left hers.

She peered at him in the reflective glass, mirroring her movements with ease. She stretched and bent and pulled and lengthened, loosened up her muscles. When he had no bar, she used his arm to balance herself as she raised first one leg and then alternated the other above her head. She had attended dance school as a youth and had won several dance competitions. She enjoyed the gracefulness choreography provided. She added Tai Chi and created her own brand of stretching movements that he fluidly kept up with. When they were warmed up, she turned to face him, looking up into those icy blue eyes of his she saw none of the warmth or passion that she observed last night which lasted into the wee hours of the morning. "I am ready if you are."

As he stood next to her, facing the mirror, he replied, "Your emotions are your worst enemy. We fight to keep fit and our reflexes sharp but that would only give you a physical chance of survival against the demon. We need to make sure he stays out of your head. I have learned a few techniques over the centuries on how to achieve inner peace and balance." He frowned at her look. "Don't mock this, Clarissa. It has saved my life on many an occasion. Follow my lead." He spread his legs wider and put the weight on his thighs. His naked upper body glistened in the pale light. Keeping his lower body still, Mel moved his arms in a wide arc in front of his face, the movements slow and controlled. "Breathing is the key. It will control your heart rate and is the core of your calm center. It will keep your emotions stable and your strength up."

Clarissa copied his motions. She added her own dexterously delicate sway to mirror him. Her control and breathing flawless in keeping her heart rate normal as she employed her martial arts instructions for a calm center. It still amazed her that she lost control of the demon because of Mel not her own past. She had buried the latter so deep down, she never thought it a concern. His coldness and mocking had set her teeth on edge and she lost focus of her thoughts, of her goal. She would never, ever let him know that he was the catalyst that almost killed her.

That he was the one who occupied her mind which infuriated her so much, she paid no attention to her surroundings until it was too late. Instead, she tried to not breathe in his scent, nor notice how his body gleamed and shimmered in the light with the sheen of sweat on his chest. She didn't think of how she would rather be licking his body than doing exercises. Then again, that was the point. To focus, to concentrate, to not be thinking of him and the way he felt around her, inside of her. Swallowing, she concentrated on his cold eyes and his movements. She reminded herself that she could do this and it would be over soon enough where she can go back to her hum-drum, monotonously boring and solitary existence.

Azamel kept his eyes focused on his own fluidity. He saw her clearly from the corner of his eye but he refused to acknowledge the tempting picture she made. Centuries of discipline taught him well. His eyes showed no emotion, his face completely composed and devoid of any expression. Her turbulent emanations reached out to him and he realized they would have a long road ahead. She affected him as strongly as he sensed her reaction to him. He had eons in which to master his constraint. Sadly, he had maybe a fortnight for her to learn at least enough to keep her alive.

After an hour of intense focus training, he turned to her and flashed a wooden staff into both their hands. "Rule, we spar only. I attack, you defend.

You attack, I defend. First one that hits flesh wins and training is over for today."

Although her mental state was slightly turbulent, one would never know by looking at her. She was stoic, composed and ready for action. She tested the weight of the staff to get used to it, twirled it around her hands and examined the balance.

"I understand."

She backed up a step as she took her stance. She watched him. Her eyes gauged his movements as to how he might come at her. He paced her, neither attacking nor defending but assessed her motions just as she did. Taking a step forward, she swung the staff to clank woodenly against his. Backing up quickly, she circled a bit more. He moved in swinging his staff and she blocked it. He spun and she blocked it again just as he pivoted with a secondary swing which she jumped over while simultaneously swinging her staff. He ducked and it missed him. They continued to thrust and parry holding each other off well.

He was impressed by her fighting skills. He had always believed that the discipline and physical wellness awarded by hard training would assist in focusing the mind. Her memories weighed her down and affected every action she made as well as every decision. She was no match for any demon physically but a fit body would help clear her thoughts and concentrate on the skills she did have. Mel decided to increase the onslaught. He could sense her becoming tired but her fighting spirit will not allow her to back down. With a smirk the executioner twisted the staff in his hands, twirled it so fast that is almost resembled a fan. He stopped the motion and kept the staff balanced horizontally between his hands. At her slightly startled look, he pounced faster than she could blink as he swept the back of her legs and pinned her to the floor, the tip of the staff a hair's breadth from her throat.

She dematerialized quickly, only to reappear behind him. She hit him in the ribs with the staff then immediately back swung to his shoulder with the other end on the other side of his body. Dropping to a squat position, she swept his feet out from under him and he quickly found himself in the same position he had her just moments before. A light sheen of sweat shimmered on her skin. He was good but she could hold her own. Holding the staff over his throat like he had done to her, she looked into his eyes. Their icy cold piercing blue was nothing like she saw just hours before and her mind flashed to him over her, his eyes dark with passion and lust. She gave her head an almost immovable shake and waited, prepared for his next move.

He grabbed the staff and used her weight as leverage as he sent her flying over his head before Mel flipped to his feet. He turned back towards her, pulled her up to stand. "Very good, Clarissa. Your reflexes have improved and your focus is better. All this practice will give you an opportunity to succeed against the demon but your main weakness is still in here." Mel poked at her chest right over the spot where her heart was located. "That is your vulnerability, which is where he will hurt you. The next step in our training will be very painful for you but crucial in order to prevail. I will meet you in the main hall after you have freshened up. I want to take a quick shower and will meet you there in thirty minutes. Well done." He gave her a slight bow." I am very satisfied with your progress."

Clarissa took his hand and let him assist her to rise. Wiping her brow, she became nervous at his poking her chest and more so at his words. As he left, she put the staff in a corner and headed back to her own room to quickly shower and meet him on time in the main hall, not at all looking forward to seeing those winged gargoyle skeletons flanking the fireplace yet again. They creeped her out but then she was sure that was why he had them there, to unhinge any guests he had.

Not giving it another thought, she stripped and entered the shower, letting the hot water glide over her silken skin. The heat from the hot water helped to loosen up her sore, tired muscles. She was fine up until that last throw he did over his head with her landing in a heap. It knocked out her breath and made some of her muscles achy. After letting the pelting water massage her tired, weary bones, she stepped out and dried off. With a towel wrapped about her slightly damp body, she started looking through her bag for her hip huggers and halter top, when her vision clouded and she became dizzy. She crumpled slightly, landing on the bed but was unaware as she was lost to the scene that intruded on her.. She sensed the stone in Xon's hands. He was trying to use it, call forth its powers and it pulled at her since she was the caretaker of the stone.

The picture unfolded in front of her. Xon stood in front of a sight she had become used to seeing the past few months since she entered a city that bustled with smells, sounds and people who took her in, willing to protect her and add her to those they considered to be under their protection.

She saw smoke coming out of the building as people evacuated and she tried to reach them to help save them. She could not move. The demon turned and looked at her. His deep rumbling voice pierced through her skull. "Give me the other half of the stone or I will see this building and all in it burned to the ground and into the fiery pits of hell." He came towards her and slashed at her with claws that were sharp and jagged. She felt pain slice through her and she screamed. How was this real? She was in the nether realm with Azamel not on the surface with Xon. Was this a dream? A vision? An alternate sense of reality? Or a combination thereof? Regardless all she knew was that she heard the demon, saw him, felt his claws though she knew she was in the room assigned to her in Mel's abode.

*****

The vision left her and her sight cleared. She was once again in her assigned quarters, lying awkwardly on the bed. Shaking her head slightly to clear it of the revelation, she moved to stand and get dressed knowing she only had a couple of minutes before Mel expected to see her in the main hall.

Finding it difficult to move, she looked down and saw the front of the towel turning red with her blood. Somehow, the demon's warning was real and the power of the partial stone he had allowed him to physically claw her. She was losing blood and she realized she was not going to make her appointment with Azamel as she collapsed back onto the bed in a sprawled out fashion.

Chapter Eleven

Mel paced the throne room, annoyed at the guardian's tardiness. *'What could be keeping the woman? It is training, not a date. She doesn't need to dress up.'* After another fifteen minutes, his annoyance won out and he stalked down the hall to her room. After several knocks produced no response, he turned the knob slowly and peeked into the room. Shock marred his features as he saw her slumped on the bed, blood staining the towel covering her otherwise naked body. Mel rushed over to her and lifted the towel slightly only to wince at the jagged marks that mutilated her flesh. Blood poured from the wounds, slowly trickled down her sides onto the mattress.

With a foul curse the judge knelt next to the bed and placed his palms over her injuries. Heat built up in within him and spread through her wounds, closed the lacerations as healing energy flowed over her skin. When she was healed, he flashed her into some clothes and softly touched her cheek. Fear for her safety, for almost losing her collided against his stubbornness. "Clarissa?" He shook her slightly to try and awaken her. "Clarissa! Please open your eyes, love."

She blinked her green eyes to pierce a stare at him and then glanced down at her belly only to see she was dressed in jeans and a shirt. Not her usual wear but? Lifting up the blouse, she looked at her unblemished, unmarred skin. "Thank you." She sat up and gazed at him with a serious concern etched on her face. "The demon is tapping into the part of the stone he has. It's not much but it is amplifying his powers somewhat. Shit, Xon used astro-projection and illusion on me. Tell me how I train for that?"

"Just because Xon used his abilities on you does not mean you cannot use yours on him. Your telekinesis and other capabilities are just as strong as his since you are the custodian of the gem he is trying to usurp. Concentration whenever he appears will enable you to be just as successful no matter the realm he appears in. Trust in yourself and you will overcome his attacks to defeat him."

She sighed as she ran her hand through her hair. "You make it sound so easy. Just focus. Just ruminate. I do but still he surprised me. It happened so fast I barely realized what was going on, much less how to attack him." Clarissa moved closer to him, fear impressed deeply on her features. "Xon was in New Orleans. He had my place of employment on fire. Was that real too? Was he killing my friends to get at me and the rest of the gem?"

Azamel frowned. "I would not put it past him. If he were able to hone in on you here in my realm then there is every possibility that what he showed you actually occurred. Remain here and I will check it out."

"No! I will go with you."

"And fall into whatever trap he has prepared for you? I warned you before that he will be anticipating you. If he came here to call you to him then he is planning on you arriving so he can get the rest of the stone. Do not be stupid, Clarissa. Not after everything you have accomplished thus far. Let me check it out. He will not be expecting me and even if, by some miracle he did think that far ahead, he cannot defeat me." Without speaking another word, Mel teleported out of the room, leaving her alone.

As she watched him depart, she screamed in fury. He left her? She knew he was probably correct but still Mel did not trust her enough to take her with him. To allow her to check on those she called friends for the last couple of months. She paced the chamber while she awaited his return.

*****

Azamel appeared outside of the bar he knew Clarissa worked at. The building was on fire. Orange, red, yellow and even some blue flames licked towards the sky. The screams of those still trapped within pierced the night. Mel remained in the shadows watching. He opened his senses to find the object of his desire. He realized that if he eliminated the threat of Xon here and now, he could get Clarissa back to her own life, away from him. No more temptation from her. No more craving her touch, her scent.

Mel frowned when he realized that Xon was not as near as he originally thought. Using his powers, Mel doused the fire from the upper floor to an exit, allowing those trapped to escape safely. He continued to watch, waited for Xon to show himself. To release the trap Mel knew was set.

Across the street, on a roof top Xon sat gazing at the chaos below. His minions waited for his command. He did not think that he had damaged the guardian that strongly during his projected visit, yet she still was not here. Who was surprised him. Although Xon could not tell exactly where the judge was, he did realize that he was near. This did not please Xon. He wanted the other part of the stone, not to have to deal with demon justice who could easily condemn him for millennia. Realizing the custodian would not appear and the joy he had originally obtained from the destruction and chaos of the fire had been depleted, Xon dismissed his men. He would find the keeper of the gem in due time. It would just take longer than planned. He gave one last look around then dematerialized as well.

Once Azamel saw all safe from the building and the fire fighters had the blaze under control, he returned to his abode. He found Clarissa anxiously awaiting him. Mel wanted nothing more than to gather her up in his arms and reassure her but he could not allow that action to occur. As she stopped pacing, she wrung her hands in front of her.

"Well?"

"The building was on fire. Everyone got out safely. The structure is damaged but not irreparable. It was a trap. I sensed him there, just could not find him directly. The power of the portion of gem he has was enough to somewhat block me, at least in pinpointing his exact location."

Clarissa sat heavily on the chair, her face in her hands and breathed deeply. "Thank you for checking on them for me. For letting me know."

"Clarissa, we are not done. You are not ready for him yet. He is still too strong, too wily." As much as Mel needed to have her gone, there was another part that did not want to see her out of his life. Not yet. Even though he knew there would come a day soon enough that he would have to set her free. He snarled to himself at how much the thought of being alone again, being without her crushed him.

She heard his growl and frowned. The coldness in his eyes indicated to her that he had no desire to have her around but did so out of some obligation to his job. "I understand and am willing to continue to learn under your guidance until you feel I am ready to confront him."

They spent the next two weeks training daily. Mel made her use the orb until she felt nothing more than a twinge of painful regret letting her past unfold before her. Her fighting skills, which were already good, became excellent and Mel admired her fortitude in working out. She even taught him a move or two and for someone as old as him, that was rather amazing. Before either realized it, she was ready and Mel knew it was time to let Xon come to them.

Chapter Twelve

They appeared in the jungle where they first met. The landscape had not changed much in the past couple of weeks. Clarissa remembered well seeing Azamel the first time leaned up against that tree. How so much had transpired between them since that day. She fell in love with him, even though she still would not admit it to him. Hell, she barely admitted it to herself. She followed him with her eyes as he set the parameters. He was unwilling to deal with Xon's henchmen so the border Mel established would keep them out.

He glanced over his shoulder on occasion to notice Clarissa. She still made his blood boil, gave him companionship. She accepted him despite the demon that resided within him. That never happened before in his life. Always the creature he contained scared any he thought about away, so he had stopped thinking about anyone and concentrated on being alone. After today however, he would never see her again and it tore him up inside. They had not touched, kissed or made love since that one night after she had healed him. He kept his distance, despite how difficult it was. He had utilized every bit of his age long discipline in order to remain stoic whenever she was around. When she was not near, Mel had put her image, scent, feel and taste aside.

Azamel had sent his minions to spread the word, discreetly of course, of where the guardian would be this day. He had been keeping track of Xon's actions and knew the demon was extremely anxious to get the stone together. So much so that he would make mistakes and that was what Mel relied on. The border set, the trap laid, Mel returned to Clarissa's side. "Are you ready?"

"Yes. As ready as I am going to be."

"I will be near. Stay focused. Stay alive." He started to move to her and steal a kiss and then thought better of it at the last moment. No need to start something that he could never finish. He refused to be weak and struggled with surrendering what he could never have. He faded out, leaving her alone in the lea.

Clarissa sat, waited for Xon to show. Although she told Azamel she was ready, being a guinea pig did not sit real well with her. She had the dagger in hand. She needed to have it here so the portion of the gem Xon had would resonate with power and indicate her location, now that she no longer had the protection of the nether realm that Mel's abode resided in. She rested against the tree in a similar pose that Mel had taken when she came across him all those weeks ago.

Minutes ticked by. Hours passed and still Xon did not show. She was getting anxious and stiff. She stood and stretched, easily slipped into the movements that she practiced over and over again with Mel during their time together. She pivoted when she found her arm grabbed and pinned behind her. Reacting on instinct, she spun, stuck her foot behind his and reversed the hold. She twisted again slightly and flipped her attacker over her shoulder to land at her feet.

Xon sputtered as he sent an energy bolt towards her. Clarissa dove, landing near the tree that supported her back only a short time ago. She quickly rose to her feet, her mouth slightly agape at the monstrous demon that stood where she was just moments before. Xon was huge, eight and a half feet tall and pure muscle, with puckish green skin, a sharp barbed tail and brown pointed horns. He sensed her gaze and his bright yellow eyes turned towards her. She swallowed at the imposing figure he made.

Guardian and demon stared at each other for a moment. Then Xon spoke, his voice resonated through the woods, "You can beg, you can plead, you can say please as much as you want. You're not getting it back, Guardian."

She looked at him, trying to find her voice, before her fury boiled over at the damage he had done thus far. Her friends, her place of employment all put into danger because of his greed. She stood before him with resolve, strength and stubbornness. "I will do none of the above. You stole my property and you will give it back, dead or alive. The choice is yours."

Xon laughed. "Then I choose death, yours!"

Xon threw a fire ball at her which she dove to dodge, only to land near his tail. He slashed the barbed appendage at her and it sliced across her chest, her blouse shredded. The barbs were poisonous and she felt the toxin seep into her open wounds as it slowly paralyzed her. She struggled and her breathing became raspy as the demon slashed at her again. She deflected his tail the second time and stabbed his ribs with her weapon, giving him a deep cut. The first bout of venom oozed into her body, weakened her and Clarissa knew she would be unable to avoid his next attack until she was unexpectedly pulled back out of harm's way.

Mel flashed in front of Xon as he gave the demon a foul glare as fear for Clarissa ripped through him. "Stay away from her! What the fuck is it with you assholes? Do you have some book on demons that states you all have to be fuck ass ugly and stink to high heaven? No amount of bleach can get rid of that."

Xon gaped at him. He would have been fearful of the judge if not for the partial power of the gem that was still within his clutches. "Fine then you can die first and she can watch as I take you out."

"Close your mouth, your breath is even worse than your stench."

The executioner lifted both hands and before the demon could move he sent an energy blast that caused Xon to fly fifty feet away into a group of trees and shrubs. Mel did not stop to see where he ended up as he went to check on Clarissa worriedly. Waving his hand over her wounds, he healed her, pulling all of the toxin out of her body.

She was still breathing heavily, trying to recuperate from the poison, yet grateful to him for his assistance. She scrambled unsteadily to her feet and stood beside him as Xon stormed back towards them. Both Mel and Clarissa prepared themselves for battle and her vision was dead on. Standing next to the handsome stranger fighting the demon to retrieve the stone as it was foreseen.

Clarissa used her telekinesis and called to the portion of the gem that Xon had, watching as it came to her. Xon tried to grab it back into his possession but Mel tackled him to keep him away from the stone and the guardian. Although immensely smaller than the demon, Mel was ancient power. He was not called the executioner for nothing. In the blink of an eye, Xon was down on his knees as Mel grabbed his neck in a vice like grip, squeezing slowly. The voice that left Mel's lips reverberated, a deep demonic sound echoing through the clearing, "You have been found guilty for several crimes, the least of which was hurting the guardian. Your sentence is death."

Before Clarissa could even take another breath, a bloodied head rolled at her feet as Xon's body toppled over. She jumped back slightly, tucking the portion of the stone the demon had found away before Mel stalked slowly towards her. She watched the executioner, uncertain yet afraid he no longer had a reason to stay and would leave her or cast her out. Or would he try taking the stone from her now that he had no excuse to remain for Xon and protect her? Could she let him go without telling him how she felt about him? She was in love with him. She loved the way he growled, infuriated, cared and forced her to come to terms with what was inside her heart as well as what she wanted.

She would die for the protection of the gem of power but she wanted a life not just an existence. Most of all she desired to spend her days and better yet, her nights with this demon she should detest, fear but instead loved with all her being. She was terrified that he would walk out of her world and she would never see him again without his ever knowing how much she cared for him.

Mel did not stop as he approached her. Instead, he pulled her to him, capturing her lips passionately with his. Azamel knew right then and there he needed her. He wanted her and could not be without her near him. After centuries of being alone, of not caring about anyone or anything, this little slip of a wolf affected him, broke through his barriers as none had before. He had thought her lost to him when Xon poisoned her and the very idea almost brought him to his knees in despair.

Every concern he had felt, every fear he had dissolved as he felt her arms wrap around his neck and she held him close to her, returned his passion with a heat of her own. He pulled back momentarily, his voice husky and low, "You are coming home with me. You still need to be trained and you need to be protected and I will do both. If you let me, tell me no now and I will leave you alone forever." Mel swallowed as apprehension of her answer enveloped his entire being.

It took her a moment to get her head wrapped around everything but the one thing she was sure of was she wanted to be with Azamel. She had nothing else to go back to, no one who wanted her, except him. And for once, she desired something for herself. "Do not leave me, Azamel. I need you." She paused, unsure if she could continue and yet realizing she needed him to know. "I love you."

Azamel released a breath he had not even realized he was holding until it expelled from his lungs He smiled as he bent down to scoop her into his arms. "I love you as well, Clarissa, and I will be by your side for as long as you will have me. Longer even, for I do not think I could ever let you go now. The thought of saying goodbye to you touched a part of me that I have not felt in eons. I did not believe I could feel ever again. You have awakened something inside of me and I cannot give you up."

Cradled in his arms, she hugged him tightly as he flashed them both back to his place in the Nether Realm, where he could keep her and the stone safe.

ABOUT THE AUTHOR

Ms. Hawks has always been interested in writing in some form or other. A few years back, she was involved with and then ran a Star Trek Interactive Writing Group which was successful for a number of years. Yes, she is a trekker and proud of it.

She has directed tours around the country and continues to do so to pay the bills. Maybe one day, she can travel for fun and let the books she writes pay the bills instead. She can only hope.

Some years back, she received her Master's Degree in Ancient Civilizations, Native American History and United States History.

It was at this time she got involved in role playing on FaceBook, which gave her ample opportunities to grow and hone her writing ability.

Taking the leap forward, she decided to try her hand at writing a novel entitled Demon's Kiss.

A sequel to Demon's Kiss, entitled Demon's Dream is available

She has a couple of other projects underway, including a new series that utilizes Native American history and mythos incorporated into her paranormal world.

Coming soon: Shifter's Hope

More From Laura Hawks

31074460R00116

Made in the USA
Middletown, DE
18 April 2016